"He's [...]ed.
"Droo[...] oy murmured. The thought was [...], out she wouldn't tell him, wouldn't give him that kind of guilt to carry around. She might have lost her heart to him, but she wouldn't lose her pride as well.

"Drooling?" Gabriel asked.

Joy glared at the fairies. Gabriel was going to think she was nuts. "We don't love each other and I don't think the, er, physical end of a relationship can be satisfying for either of us without it."

"Come on, Joy. You know you want to jump his bones," Blossom said.

"Blossom," the other two fairies gasped.

"What?" The yellow fairy asked innocently. "She does."

"There are reasons we should marry, but, like all marriages-of-convenience, there's no reason to force ourselves to become physical. It's business, pure and simple."

"That's it, Joy. Make the man admit he loves you first," Fern cheered.

"Force ourselves?" Gabriel took a step closer, an ominous look in his eyes.

Joy side-stepped, not wanting to touch him, knowing she wouldn't be able to say no again if they did. Gabriel's momentum carried him forward and since Joy had moved, he leaned into what should have been the window, but wasn't since it was still open. He slipped forward, the top half of him falling out onto the porch roof.

"Gabriel!" she shouted, grabbing the waistband of his boxer shorts.

Slowly, he rose and pulled Joy's hand from his pants. "The next time you put your hand down there I hope you're intending to take me for a fall, not save me from one."

To my grandmother, Marion Morrow—"Nana"—who always kept me well supplied with books and dreams.

And to Jean Allue, an adopted Grandmother of my heart, who's cheered me on as I chased those dreams.

Other Books by Holly Fuhrmann

Mad About Max
Miracles for Nick (coming in 2001)

MAGIC FOR JOY

✱✱✱

Holly Fuhrmann

The sale of this book without its cover is unauthorized. If you purchased this book without a cover, you should be aware that it was reported to the publisher as "unsold and destroyed." Neither the author nor the publisher has received payment for the sale of this "stripped book."

MAGIC FOR JOY

Published by ImaJinn Books, a division of ImaJinn

Copyright © November, 2000 by Holly Fuhrmann

Printed and bound in the United States of America. All rights reserved. No part of this book may be reproduced in any form or by any means (electronic, mechanical, photocopying, recording, or otherwise) without prior written permission of both the copyright holder and the above publisher of this book, except by a reviewer, who may quote brief passages in a review. For information, address: ImaJinn Books, a division of ImaJinn, P.O. Box 162, Hickory Corners, MI 49060-0162; or call toll free 1-877-625-3592.

ISBN: 1-893896-19-6

10 9 8 7 6 5 4 3 2 1

PUBLISHER'S NOTE:
This book is a work of fiction. Names, characters, places and incidents are products of the author's imagination or are used fictitiously. Any resemblance to actual events or locales or persons, living or dead, is entirely coincidental.

Books are available at quantity discounts when used to promote products or services. For information please write to: Marketing Division, ImaJinn Books, P.O. Box 162, Hickory Corners, MI 49060-0162, or call toll free 1-877-625-3592.

Cover design by Rickey Mallory

ImaJinn Books, a division of ImaJinn
P.O. Box 162, Hickory Corners, MI 49060-0162
Toll Free: 1-877-625-3592
http://www.imajinnbooks.com

One

"Joy."

Joy paused and looked behind her. The only thing that met her eye was the empty, unfamiliar room she'd been assigned for the duration of the house-party. Despite the chills climbing up her spine, she forced herself to return to her unpacking.

All day long she'd felt like she was being watched, which was absurd. Who on Earth would want to watch her? She gave a little laugh. No one. That was the answer. She was boringly normal, not the type of woman to inspire anyone to follow her. Five feet and three inches of well-padded normalcy. No chestnut curls or azure eyes. Nope. Just straight brown hair and blue eyes. Normal. No secret admirers, no stalkers. Not for Joy Aaronson.

"Joy."

She jumped and whirled around. This time the room wasn't empty. Three elderly ladies stood side-by-side, watching her. No, not just watching, they were studying her. Joy's mouth was suddenly as dry as the Sahara, and the chills blew Arctic against her backbone.

"I'm sorry, you must have the wrong room."

The trio smiled in unison. It might have been endearing if the entire situation wasn't so eerie. She hadn't heard the door open, hadn't heard a sound.

Joy took in her uninvited guests. They were small women, smaller than Joy herself. None of them could be over four and a half feet tall. They were in their mid-fifties, Joy would guess. A redhead was sporting a sequined red dress with stiletto-heeled shoes that belonged on someone thirty years her junior. A brunette wore a green, Orient-inspired dress. And a blonde—whose hair was a hideous shade of yellow that belonged on a canary not on a human—was wearing a buttercup gown that would have looked at home with Scarlet O'Hara on Tara.

The trio was as extraordinarily different as Joy was ordinary to the point of boring. They were the type that might attract a stalker.

Joy smiled sympathetically. There was no use alienating the weird trio when she planned to beg favors from them later. "The maid showed me up to this room, so I'm pretty sure I'm in the right one. You might want to go check with her. She'll be able to point you all in the right direction."

"Joy, we're not in the wrong room by mistake," said the brunette.

"We don't make mistakes," said the blonde. The redhead shot her a funny look, and the blonde hastily added, "Well, not often." Another red-raised eyebrow. "Okay, maybe we make mistakes, but they all turn out right in the end. And we're not mistaken about the room, or who's in it. We're looking for you."

"Girls, I suggest you allow me to make our introductions." The redhead was obviously accustomed to taking charge. "Joy, we know about Ripples, and that's one of the reasons we're here, to see to it this fund-raising party is successful."

Ripples was Joy's non-profit foundation that funded a number of small charities. She'd realized years ago she couldn't change the world, but Ripples was Joy's attempt to change small corners of it.

"Ripples can use all the friends, and all the help with fund-raising, we can get." Raising money for Ripples was the reason Joy was attending this upscale house party, and though she welcomed their help, something about these three women still made her nervous. "I'm glad Mrs. St. John has already started to spread the word about the foundation and what we do."

"Actually, she didn't. At least not that we know of. You see, we're friends of your brother. Actually we knew Grace first, but we've come to know and love Max as well."

Joy sank to the bed, blatantly staring at the three. Friends of Grace's? Grace was a romance author who wrote about three bumbling fairy godmothers. Godmothers who... now that Joy stopped and thought about it... these women were dressed exactly like. A simple explanation occurred to her.

"Is this party a costume one? How wonderful of you to dress up like Grace's fairy godmothers. Did Trudi tell you I was coming? If everyone's costume is as great as yours, I'm going to stick out like a sore thumb. I just brought a cocktail dress."

"Darling, you obviously don't know Trudi." The brunette shook her head. "She would never do anything as crass as holding a costume party."

"And if she did we'd come as something other than ourselves." The blonde turned to her companions. "Do you remember Leila's party? I so enjoy the can-can costumes. We could go in those again."

"There is no costume party," the redhead reminded her.

"Oh."

Seeing the blonde's face fall in disappointment, Joy almost wished there was a costume party. "Maybe next time," she offered softly.

The older woman's smile was as bright as her banana-colored hair.

"Ladies, I'm sorry. I still don't understand what I can do for you."

The blonde and brunette looked as if they were about to say something, but the redhead held up a hand, silencing them. "I've told you two over and over again, let me handle these initial meetings. All you do with your chatter is confuse our goddaughters."

"Goddaughter?" Joy's smile drooped a bit, and a faint headache began to stir behind her eyes.

The redhead nodded encouragingly. "Joy, you see, we're

here to help you."

"Help me raise money for Ripples?"

"Oh, no. We're here to help you find your own true love," the redhead said as the other two bobbed their heads in agreement. "We're your fairy godmothers."

Joy tried to laugh. This was some joke. Max must be behind it.

Despite his doctorly occupation, he had always enjoyed tormenting her, trying to convince her that she needed his psychiatric help. "Okay, you three. The joke's over. Tell my dear brother, Max, it didn't work."

"Dear, we're not joking." The redhead did indeed look deadly serious. "We've been watching you for quite sometime."

Obviously not able to remain silent, the brunette piped in, "And we know..."

The blonde cut her off. "Yes, we know that you're not happy. You're missing something."

The two took off, bouncing sentences right after the other's.

"You're missing a good man—"

"Not that we're saying you need a man to make you complete—"

"Certainly not. This is the new millennium, and women have learned to stand on their own two feet—"

"And you've done a great job—"

"But you need—"

"Yes, you need something more—"

"*Someone* more—"

"And we're—"

"Girls." The redhead had had enough. The two shut up.

Joy was grateful. Trying to watch the two of them as they talked had been like trying to watch a high speed tennis ball fly back and forth on the court. Her headache was going to be complicated by a stiff neck.

"Now," said the redhead, once again in charge of the very odd, probably crazy, trio. Maybe they were three of Max's patients, escapees from some asylum. Did they even have asylums anymore?

"Joy." The redhead pulled her from her ruminations. "We

realize that this is all confusing, but we know you've read Grace's books, so we know you know how this works. In case you hadn't guessed, I'm Myrtle." Myrtle gestured to the blonde. " She is Blossom, and this is Fern." The brunette nodded.

"We've been looking for your Mr. Right for quite some time, and we've finally found him," Blossom said in a rush.

"The problem was he didn't really look like a *right*..." Fern interrupted. "More like a wrong. There were quite a few strikes against."

"But there was the wish to consider," Blossom said.

"And you would be an answer to one, despite the strikes against the other," Fern said.

"Helen, for instance," Blossom muttered.

"Plus he was badly burned by—"

"Girls." The sisters were silent. "Suffice to say, that despite some hurdles that will have be to overcome, we have found the perfect man for you. And despite the problems you might have to face, you know we'll be right beside you every step of the way."

It was too much. Joy didn't know if she should take some aspirin—or maybe a Valium— or call Max for a reference. Maybe she should call Grace, since the trio claimed to be her brainchildren. The tempo of her headache picked up speed as she considered what she should do next. Were the three women the crazy ones, or was she? "I don't understand what precisely is going on, but I wish you'd all leave. I have an important party—"

"Full of important people with deep pockets," Blossom said, nodding as if she knew what was going on.

"I can't deal with this joke. Tell Max I said, *Ha, Ha*."

"Sweetheart, we'll let you get ready for your party, but we'll be back to talk to you soon." The redhead, Myrtle, smiled. "We just wanted to drop in and say hello before the fun begins."

The three disappeared in the blink of an eye. They were either very quiet and *very* quick, or they were really fairy—

Joy shut off the thought. She would be crazy if she believed they were fairy godmothers. And crazy is just what Max, and his sick sense of humor, wanted her to think she was, so she wouldn't. She was going to take some aspirin, get dressed and go to this party. And reach into all those lovely deep pockets, taking as much money as possible for Ripples. And, most of all, she was going to forget this odd scene had ever been played out.

That's exactly what she was going to do.

***

Half an hour later she strode down the hall—dressed, headache numbed by aspirin—with her mind on the party, *not* on the fairies. She wasn't going to think about them, she told herself over and over as she did just that. A physical jolt pulled her from her sanity impairment worries.

"Darn!" she swore.

It was the only word Joy could manage as she began the long descent to the floor. The noise was loud. The clattering of plates was accompanied by the tinkling of silverware and the shattering of glasses.

Joy landed on her well-padded rump and sat momentarily stunned, surrounded by the remains of what must have been the dinner's appetizers. She'd done it again. Actually, she hadn't done it this time. It was a combination of fairy befuddlement and the small form in a blue jumper huddled against the wall.

"Are you okay?" Joy simultaneously asked the woman who had been carrying the tray and the little girl who had instigated the three-way collision.

Two red braids bobbed with the rhythm of the girl's nodding head, but no words escaped her.

"I'm just fine," said the woman. "But if her," she jerked her hand toward the girl, "mother finds out what just happened there will be..."

"It was an accident," Joy told the woman firmly. "Everyone has accidents. Since all three of us are okay, I guess our only casualties are a few plates and glasses." Joy smiled at the little girl, but there was no answering expression. The child stood motionless, soundlessly surveying the damage.

From her inelegant seat on the floor, Joy was in the perfect position to pick up the pieces, and she did so.

"Now, you might think that this bumping was a fluke..."

Joy glanced toward the woman and waited for her to supply her name.

"Martha," the woman finally said.

"Martha. If that's what you think, why, then you have another think coming. I'm here to tell you that if it hadn't been the two of you, it would have been something else. I seem to have the ability to fall over nothing."

Though she was talking to Martha, Joy kept her eye on the little girl. "Why, just the other day I was licking an envelope, sending a letter to my brother, and the paper cut my tongue. Can you imagine? A paper cut on your tongue? Hurt like the dickens. Now it takes an especially klutzy person to paper cut their tongue... the type of person who goes tripping over little girls who are only doing what little girls are supposed to do."

Martha gave a reluctant snort, and what might have been the beginning of a smile flitted across her face.

Joy glanced over her shoulder, but the child still had a look of terror in her eyes. "Didn't you know that everything in the world has a purpose? Children are here to run and scream and laugh and make messes. Older brothers are here to torment sisters."

Thinking of her older brothers reminded her of Max and momentarily brought the three supposed fairies to mind. For a split second Joy thought she saw them standing just behind the little girl, but in the next blink of her eyes she was once again alone with Martha and the silent child.

Now she was seeing things. It was all Max's fault. She had no idea how he'd bribed three strange women into playing along with his joke, but he was going to pay... and pay big. "But any self-respecting sister knows how to outsmart brothers."

She looked up again at the little girl. "Do you have any brothers or sisters?"

Braids swaying, the little girl shook her head.

"Do you have a name?"

A shy nod this time. "Sophie. Mother hates the way that sounds. She's the only one who calls me Sophia, but really I'm just plain old Sophie." The words were soft, hesitant, but it was a start.

Joy scratched her chin and looked at the child with mock consideration. "I think you're right. You're definitely a Sophie. A Sophia would be a quiet mouse of a girl who didn't do anything but sit in a corner all day. I can tell you're the kind of girl who likes to run and shout. Why, I even believe you might be the kind of girl who likes to go fishing." Despite her own problems... pseudo-fairies and practical joking brothers... Joy couldn't resist trying to ease a smile onto the child's face.

Her need to save the world was one of the many problems Max was forever hounding her about. But Joy didn't think it truly qualified as a problem. She didn't like to see people who were hurting or unhappy. Neither did Max. He tried to heal the world with psychiatry—by poking around in people's brains. Joy preferred working at making people's lives better, so maybe they'd learn to find their happiness on their own.

Sophie shook her head. "I've never fished. Mama thinks I should be a Sophia."

Joy dramatically looked the girl over. "Well, I've studied these things for many years, and I can tell you that you most certainly aren't the kind of girl to stay in a corner for too long. What does your Daddy say?"

"He doesn't say anything."

Joy's heart broke, more for what she heard behind the words than because of the words themselves. "Well, I do, and I know. I was the kind of girl who was always getting in trouble. I can tell a kindred spirit when I see one."

"What's a kindred spirit?" Sophie took a step towards Joy.

"Someone who knows how you feel."

Sophie looked thoughtful. "Then you're my kindred spirit, too."

"I thought so." Joy and Martha had finished putting the evidence of the disaster back on the tray. "Now, I have to take this back and see if I can help Martha find something else to serve. But maybe you could meet me in the kitchen tomorrow after breakfast, and we can see about teaching you how to fish."

"Do you mean it?" Sophie asked, doubt in her eyes.

"My dear, kindred spirit, you should know right now, I never say anything I don't mean." She struggled from her knees to

her feet, tray in hand, ignoring Martha's attempts to take it.
"Now, I'll see you tomorrow in the kitchen half an hour after breakfast. And don't wear a frilly dress. Jeans and a t-shirt are what you're going to need."
A smile burst out on the little girl's face. "I'll see you in the morning."
Joy started back into the kitchen, warmed by Sophie's smile. Martha gave her a strange look, but didn't try to take the tray again.
"Are you really going fishing with the girl?"
"It appears that I am."
That hint of a smile once again playing across her face, Martha said, "Well, I guess I could be persuaded to pack a lunch."
"Peanut butter and jelly?"
Martha gave her another odd look. "Just who are you? You're not anything like Mrs. St. John's normal guests."
"Martha, you've learned the truth so quickly. I'm not anyone's normal anything." Joy laughed and Martha joined in, her face covered in a broad smile, not just a hint of one.
"So what are we going to do about an appetizer? Mrs. St. John strikes me as the type that will expect everything just so, no excuses," Joy asked, purposely using *we*, not *you*.
"Then it's lucky for us this disaster struck before we served the entree. Instead of salad, I'll thaw some consumé in the microwave and serve that. Her-high-and-mightiness will never know the difference."
"What do you know about Sophie?" Joy asked. She brushed the remains of the salad, broken shards and all, into the trash.
"Now, there's a sad story. That little girl is a casualty of greed. The missus and her ex fought long and hard over custody of poor Miss Sophia. The missus won, and Sophia moved here last year. She's a quiet one, forever lurking about the shadows, which is just how Ms. St. John likes it.
"As a matter of fact, today's accident was the first bit of fluster the child has caused in the entire year she's been here. She mainly stays in her rooms with her nanny." As she spoke, Martha bustled about the kitchen, a flurry of motion.

"You can't blame this accident on Sophie." No, Joy was going to blame Max and Grace and Grace's fairies. "I was lost in thought and hurrying down the hall... a deadly combination. To be honest, accidents seem to find me all on their own." Joy had long ago come to accept that particular foible about herself.

The way she looked at it, there were things that could change, and then there were things a person was just stuck with. Accidents were one of the latter.

Thinking of the accident reminded her of fishing. She was going to have to sneak out and buy some poles. She'd seen a great pond about a mile from the St. John home, so a fishing hole was no problem.

Martha began to refill the tray. "Ms. St. John is probably wondering where you are."

"Rats," Joy cried, already racing from the kitchen. "Sorry again, Martha."

She hurried down the hall. She wasn't looking forward to this meal, but it went with the job. Catching her breath outside the formal dining room doors, Joy smoothed her hair and took a deep breath.

Think of the job, not fairies or unhappy little girls, she warned herself. The three fairy impostors were probably in that room, friends of Max's. They'd played that horrible prank. Now she was going to guilt them out of a bunch of money. No one at Trudi St. John's party was without a bunch of the green stuff, but when they left that night, Joy intended on seeing they left with lighter purses.

She entered the dining room, determined no more disasters would come her way this day. She'd be charming. She'd be sweet. She would not be clumsy. Charming and sweet meant money, and Ripples needed the money.

***

The party had gone well, but that hadn't stopped Joy from spending her night tossing and turning. She sipped her coffee, praying that some reasonable explanation of yesterday's fairy visit would present itself. There had been no short, bright-haired women at the party. When she'd asked Trudi, the woman had just given her an odd look and replied she didn't know anyone who fit the description.

To make matters worse, when she'd climbed wearily back to her room, determined to drive to a twenty-four hour store to buy poles, there had been two fishing poles at the end of her bed. *Martha.* That was the only explanation. Or at least, it was the only explanation Joy wanted to accept. But when she'd asked the cook at breakfast, the answer had been no.

It couldn't be fairies. There was no such thing. Only someone certifiably insane would believe in fairy godmothers.

Joy didn't feel insane. As a matter of fact, she was the most practical person in her family. No, she wasn't insane. And for the life of her, she couldn't decide how Max could have orchestrated the fairies, or why he would have.

Joy's worries took backseat as she sensed, more than heard, someone else enter the room. Without turning she said, "Good morning, Sophie. I hope you remembered to dress for the fish. They don't like to be caught by anyone too fancy."

She turned. Sophie stood against the wall, tentative smile on her face. Her hair was in neat little braids, and she wore a crisp pair of jeans and a designer polo shirt. "Mother threw away all my t-shirts," she said. "Is this okay?"

Joy could see the fear of rejection in those beautiful little brown eyes. She gave her best reassuring smile. "You look just right. Not too messy, not too fancy. The fish will love you." She stood. "Are you ready?"

Sophie nodded.

"Well, then, let's get this show on the road."

Two bluegill later, they sat flicking their poles in the water. "Won't Mother be mad if she finds you're out here?"

Joy laughed. "I doubt she'll notice as long as I'm back in time for lunch."

"But if she did, she might not give you your money," Sophie continued stubbornly.

"Maybe. But I've gotten money out of tighter pockets than hers, so don't worry." Joy laughed. Being a first-rate klutz and money machine wouldn't have seemed to go hand in hand, but Joy had found a way to combine her talents, much to her family's dismay. With Max being a psychiatrist, and her brother Nick a lawyer, Joy didn't think she'd ever find a comfortable spot for herself. Eventually she'd found her niche, maybe not as prestigious as her brothers, but it was hers and she liked it.

"Really, it's nothing to worry about," Joy said with a smile.

Despite her obvious worry, Sophie smiled back. "Let's go back anyway."

"Okay, you slave driver, you win." They reeled in their lines, and the fish were placed in a little bucket. They walked back towards the house with a slow, lazy gait.

"I miss my daddy," Sophie said out of the blue.

"I'm sure he misses you, too."

Sophie nodded. "Mother wouldn't."

"I'm sure your mother loves you." How could anyone not love this sweet little girl?

Sophie's brows drew together, unsure. "Maybe."

Joy dropped the poles and knelt down. "Listen to me. Your mother might not be the most motherly mom I've ever seen, but sometimes that happens. That doesn't mean she doesn't love you.

"It sounds like your dad loves you lots too, and I'm sure you'll be with him again. And you have me, a kindred spirit, someone to understand and hug you."

So saying, Joy swept the child into her embrace. For once her ample padding stood her in good stead. It cushioned the fragile spirit she hugged tight. "You and I are going to be great friends."

"But you won't stay. When Mother's given you the money today, you'll leave."

"The thing with kindred spirits is they never are far apart." She hugged the girl again. They made their way back up to the house.

For a moment, Joy almost wished the three women from yesterday really were fairy godmothers. If they were real, she'd wish that Sophie would have a family and feel loved, really loved.

"Done," a voice seemed to whisper in her head. Joy turned around, expecting to see someone walking behind her and Sophie, but all she saw was Trudi St. John's well-manicured lawn,

framed by the woods in the background.
A small shiver climbed her spine, but Joy pushed it aside. She was not going to allow Max's weird sense of humor to spook her.

***

Joy sat in a chaise lounge poolside, across from her hostess. Her bags were packed, and she was ready to hit the road. The party had been a huge success. The funds she'd raised by rubbing shoulders with Trudi St. John's friends would keep Ripples running for a few more months anyway. Though she'd kept Ripples in the black, Joy didn't feel a sense of accomplishment. She was leaving with money, but she was leaving behind the saddest set of brown eyes she'd ever seen.

Last night she'd learned that Trudi St. John's eyes were as hard as her daughter's were sad. Joy forced herself to smile as she said, "Thank you again for hosting the event. Ripples will be able to do a lot with the money your guests contributed."

"I haven't had a chance to talk to you about my donation." Trudi leaned forward.

Joy felt distinctly uneasy. Trudi was making her feel hunted. "You've already done so much. But Ripples, and all the people it helps, will be happy to let you do more."

"Yes, well, I have a small request to make of you before I write my check. You see, I need someone to take Sophie to her father's. William proposed last night, you see." She flashed a huge diamond ring.

Joy didn't need to be an expert in gems to realize how expensive the ring was. But expense didn't necessarily equal passion. She remembered William from last night. The term "cold fish" came to mind.

"He's adamant that we marry as soon as possible. His business takes him all over the world, and he wants me at his side. Marcie, the child's nanny, refuses to make the trip to take Sophie to her father. He lives in Erie, Pennsylvania and I don't have time to go that far. William wants to leave as soon as possible. And it's not as if I can take a child with me."

"Are you asking me if I would consider taking Sophie to her father?" *What kind of woman would entrust a job like that to a virtual stranger?*

Trudi, who was sprawled in the chaise lounge, lowered her sunglasses and peered at Joy over their rims. "I wasn't exactly asking. I was bargaining. I know Ripples needs my support..."

"And in order to gain that support, you think I'll take a child I hardly know to a man I've never met?"

"I think you're a woman who understands back scratching," Trudi said, slipping her glasses back over her eyes.

"You aren't hesitant about letting your little girl travel with a stranger?" Joy knew if she had a girl as precious as Sophie, she would never let her go with just anyone.

"Hardly that. I've known Nick for years, and I think I've even met Max once or twice." Trudi tapped her beautifully manicured nails on the arm of the chair. "And I've followed your work through them, and through some other acquaintances. That's why I decided to host this fund-raiser. And of course we've gotten to know each other while we worked on this project. You're a better choice than just sticking Sophia on a plane and letting her make the trip on her own."

"I just don't know," Joy hedged, though she knew she was going to say yes. If she said no, who would Trudi palm Sophie off on then?

"Then you won't do it?" Obviously unused to being denied, shock registered on Trudi's face.

Joy crossed her fingers behind her back, hoping she was playing this hand right. "I'd be happy to take Sophie to her father. This is a permanent move, isn't it?"

Trudi nodded. "William's business takes him all over the world. Naturally, I'll travel with him. As I said before, it would be impossible to take a child with me."

Joy held her smile inside, gripping it with the fiercest control she'd ever exercised. "Well, can you have the papers ready by the time we leave?"

"Papers?" Trudi looked confused.

"Of course. If Mr. St. John is taking over permanent care of Sophie, he'll need all the legal forms signed and witnessed. What if something happened to her, and you couldn't be reached, traveling like you're planning? He needs to be the custodial parent on paper."

"I'll call my lawyer and have him draw them up. I'm sure he can fax over the proper documents."

"He'd take care of it that fast?"

Trudi just laughed. "Honey, remember the old saying money talks? Well, it doesn't just talk, it shouts." Joy almost wished the fairy godmothers were real, so she could thank them. Sophie was going back to her father. The child spoke with affection about him, and Joy couldn't imagine he'd be a worse parent than Trudi.

Her little kindred spirit was going to be removed from this stifling, oppressive atmosphere. Joy wanted to laugh and dance for the sheer happiness that welled within her heart.

"I'll have Ripples' check ready along with Sophie and her things by tomorrow," Trudi added, coming to the end of her monologue about William and all the things they were going to do.

"That would be wonderful."

"I'll have directions to Gabriel's, and money to cover your expenses for the trip," Trudi added.

"That would be fine. Have you told Sophie yet?"

"Oh, why don't you see if you can track her down? Tell her I'll be up later to say goodbye."

Joy left then, turned her back to conceal the smile she just couldn't hold in any longer. Anger warred with her sense of accomplishment. Sophie was a treasure, one that Trudi had never recognized. Joy only prayed that Gabriel St. John would.

Still smiling, she ran down the hall of the cold mansion, looking for Sophie.

"Joy."

She knew before she turned around that they were back. She turned, but instead of the three fake-fairy ladies, only one stood in the quiet hall.

"Myrtle?"

"I'm glad you found the poles this morning. That trip was just what Sophie needed. We were worried about how to get her back to her father. But she likes you. She'll go with no fuss."

"You set this up?"

"Of course we did. You made a wish, remember?"

"But..."

"Joy, I know you're still trying to think of a rational explanation. Rational seems to be something you Aaronson's excel at. You've tried everything from blaming Max to thinking you're nuts. Grace had a hard time at first as well, and she created us."

"You're not real." No one in the twenty-first century had fairy godmothers...Myths, fairy tales, that's all they were. "You're not real," she repeated, though she wasn't sure whether she was trying to convince herself or Myrtle.

"As real as you are, in our own way. I left my sisters behind because sometimes they can be a little much."

Joy couldn't help the smile that tugged at her lips.

Myrtle's smile echoed hers. "Okay, we can all be a bit much. It's Grace's fault, really. We were created in her imagination. Now, about what we're going to do next. I think it would be easier if we could just get past all the mental doubts, and thoughts of brotherly jokes and mental instability. Call Max and Grace."

"Call them?"

"Before you leave with Sophie, call them. Ask them how they got together."

"I don't have to ask. Grace had problems with some characters and went to Max for his psychiatric opinion and..." Joy stopped. "You three were the problem?"

"Grace seemed to worry that she was sanity-impaired when we showed up. Just call them, and we can get past that nonsense." Myrtle disappeared as quickly and quietly as she had yesterday.

Call Grace and Max? How would she start, *Max, I'm seeing fairies...*

Two

"Yes."

Joy had waited until later in the day when she was pretty sure she was fairy-free to call her brother. She expected a variety of reactions to her *are the fairies real* question, but not this. She removed the telephone receiver from her ear and stared at it in disbelief. Bringing it back to her ear, she said, "Max?"

"I said, the answer is yes. It sounds insane—and believe me, I should know—but there it is. They're real. And they're not going to leave until you're married to your own-true-love."

"Max, this is insane."

"I already said that. I agree. But sometimes, Joy, you just have to take things on faith. I don't have to see them to believe in them. I know they're real. You have the advantage of seeing them, and you have to face the fact that you have three fairy godmothers. They were Grace's characters, then they came to life—if you ask, they'll tell you how, though I don't claim to understand any of it. But just because I can't explain it doesn't mean I don't believe in them."

"This is some huge joke, and I know there's a punch line somewhere. I just haven't figured it out."

"Don't try. It's no joke. Like I said, it's crazy, but it's real. *They are real.*"

"Max, you can't expect me to buy this."

"Grace and I did our time, and you're going to have to do

yours. All I can hope is that Nick is next. I'm going to love watching him survive the fairies' help."

"Survive?" The word sounded ominous.

"Listen, Joy, I've got to run. The baby's crying. Talk to you soon."

"Max, don't you dare..." There was a distinct click. "...hang up on me." Joy sat staring at the phone in her hand. She'd expected her brother to tell her to rush home and start some heavy drug regimen, but to have him say the fairies were real?

"As real as you are."

Joy turned around, and the three stood there smiling at her. "And you've got to be on the road. It's only a four or five hour drive, and Sophie needs to get home."

"I don't understand any of this."

"You will," Fern promised her.

Joy eyed them suspiciously. "You're not coming on the trip with us, are you?"

Blossom glanced at her sisters before answering. "That wouldn't be wise."

"Why?"

"Ah, there's a small complication in your case," Blossom admitted.

"Complication?" Max's oblique warning came to mind, and Joy's stomach sank.

"She's repeating what you say. That's not a good sign," Fern said.

"Girls." Myrtle, the voice of reason.

Joy tried to steady her voice. "Myrtle, what's going on?"

"Now, now, it's not as bad as Blossom makes it sound. You see, only our godchildren can see us."

"And?"

"And sometimes children. We wouldn't want to startle Sophie. She's been through enough," Fern added.

"We've decided to try to be a bit more circumspect, is what the girls are trying to say. So, unless it's an emergency, we'll avoid talking to you in public." Myrtle smiled, as if her comments should make Joy feel better.

All Joy felt was a sinking sense of dread. "And if you think it's an emergency?"

"Then we'll take the risk," Myrtle said.

"Of me being institutionalized," Joy muttered.

"Oh, I don't think you have to worry. Max would testify to your psychological health," Blossom said.

Fern pointed to a gaudy neon green wristwatch. "You really do have to get going." The three fairies disappeared.

Joy couldn't decide if she was relieved or nervous. When they were with her, at least she knew what they were up to. And, whether they were real or not, Joy had the distinct feeling that it was best to know what they were up to at all times.

***

"We're here," Sophie shouted excitedly.

"I see. I see. We're here." Joy was thankful that summer days were so long, though this one had seemed longer than most. Finding the driveway was hard enough at dusk. It would have been impossible if it had been dark.

"Do you think Daddy's waiting for us?" Sophie asked for the thousandth time.

"I'm sure he is." Joy turned onto a pot-holed dirt driveway that led back into a grove of trees, twisting and winding. "Why, I bet he's watching out his window right now, wondering what's taking us so long."

"You drive too slow," Sophie said, not for the first time. "There it is." She pointed to the lone, rough-hewn lumber-sided house that stood in the midst of a forest of trees. Really, it was almost a cottage and much smaller than the mansion residence of Trudi St. John. But what it lacked in ostentatiousness, it gained in warmth. This was a home, a place where Sophie could be a little girl.

A giant porch circled the building's two sides that Joy could see, and she could almost picture rocking with the little girl in the swing that hung to the right of the door.

"Where's Daddy?" Sophie cried as Joy pulled to a stop. She'd unbuckled her seatbelt and was out of the truck before Joy had even turned off the ignition.

Joy felt a tug at her heart as she watched her run to the door. Used to pulling up stakes at the merest whim or shift of the breeze, Joy had never felt so much as a twinge of regret. Maybe it wasn't just the thought of leaving this precious little girl. Maybe it was partially a case of nerves. Who knew what the fairies had in store for her after this trip? She had little optimism about their matchmaking.

She'd grown up feeling like the odd duck in a pond full of swans. She'd never quite fit in, never quite belonged. And the relationships she'd been in had never worked out, not that there had been all that many. Not that many at all.

And as sweet and good-intentioned as the fairies might be, Joy doubted they'd be able to find her the type of relationship she longed for. It wasn't that she wanted much. Just a home and family, a man who wasn't just her lover, but her friend. No, that dream might not be all that much, but it was everything to her.

Sophie stood on the porch, expectancy written in every line of her body, but the door didn't open. "Daddy?"

Joy walked up onto the porch and peeked into one of the windows. No lights, no indication that anyone was home. "Looks like we're out of luck, hon. Your Daddy probably had to run to the store and thought he had more time. He'll be home soon."

"Yeah, sure," Sophie said, a huge tear perched on her eyelashes, ready to fall.

"Come here, honey." Joy knelt on the porch and opened her arms. She cushioned Sophie's head against her ample bosom. Patting the shoulders that gave telltale heaves, she whispered, "It's okay, sweetheart. He'll be here soon."

Sophie whispered, "No one wants me."

"Oh, Sophie, you couldn't be more wrong. There are so many people who love you and want you." Joy rocked the child in her embrace.

"Mother didn't love me, and now Daddy doesn't, either."

"Honey, I'm sure your daddy loves you. And your mother loves you in her own way. She is just one of those people who has a hard time showing it. She doesn't know about little girls, so she doesn't know how to show you how she feels."

Pulling away from Joy's embrace, sniffing and wiping her

nose on the hem of her shirt, she said, "You know how to show me."

Joy laughed. "That's because I have a hard time hiding anything I feel. My brother's used to laugh and say I wore my heart on my sleeve." At the child's puzzled expression, Joy explained, "Everyone always knew how my heart felt. And I love you."

"I'm your kindred spirit," Sophie said.

Joy nodded, brushing a stray lock of hair behind Sophie's ear. "You're my kindred spirit. I knew the moment we bumped into each other."

Sophie giggled through her tears. "A kindred spirit," she whispered.

Joy nodded. "After your Daddy comes home and we unpack your things, it'll be time for me to go. But wherever I go, you'll always know how much I love you."

"I don't want you to go," Sophie wailed, flinging herself back into Joy's arms.

Joy didn't want to go, either. Sophie felt so right in her arms. She'd always dreamed about being a mother, but the more time went by, the more she doubted it would ever happen. She wasn't extraordinary enough to catch a man's interest. But holding Sophie, she could imagine what it would be like to have a daughter—a daughter with brown eyes that just begged to be loved.

"Ah, honey, I explained I couldn't stay. But things will be better now. You'll be with your Daddy and have all these woods to play in. This fall you'll start school and meet all kinds of new friends. You'll forget me soon enough."

"No, I won't," Sophie told her.

Sighing, Joy hugged her tight. "And I won't forget you either."

The sun was sinking, and though it was early summer, the air beneath the trees was chilly. "Tell you what? Let's go back to the truck, and I'll pull my sleeping bag out of the back. We can cuddle on the seat and wait for your daddy. I'm sure he'll be back any minute now." She was thankful she'd driven to Trudi's fund-raiser, rather than taking a flight. The truck was always well stocked with this and that.

Sophie nodded and, clinging to Joy's hand, obediently followed her back to the truck. "Tell me a story," she whispered when they lay snuggled beneath the sleeping bag.

"Once upon a time there was a little girl named..."

"Sophie."

"And her best friend..."

"Joy."

"One day they decided to set off on an adventure..."

Joy launched into the story with gusto, sending the fictional Joy and Sophie into a magical fairyland on a quest for magic treasure. Before the fictional Joy and Sophie had confronted the terrible monster who was guarding the treasure, Sophie was sleeping. "Goodnight, sweetheart," Joy whispered as she planted a tender kiss on her forehead. "Sweet dreams."

"The child's wrong."

Joy was almost getting used to the fairies' appearances. All three fairies stood at the side of the truck, peering in through the window, concern filling their eyes. "We love her, too."

"Where is her father? You're supposed to be fairies, so why isn't he here?"

"Go to sleep, Joy." Myrtle's voice was soothing. "He'll be here when he gets here. We're magic, but we're not omnipotent. Just go to sleep. Everything will be all right." All three fairies blinked out of sight.

Instead of being reassured, the words filled Joy with dread. Staring at the stars that had begun to make their appearance through the windshield and holding the little girl tight, Joy worried about the fairies. If Max was right, she wasn't crazy and this wasn't a joke. What she *was* was in trouble. She'd read Grace's books and knew what sort of mess the fairies tended to make of their godchildren's lives.

Joy fell asleep wondering just what they had planned for her.

***

It was the pounding that woke her up. An angry-eyed man stood outside the locked driver's-side door, hammering wildly on the window.

"Sh," Joy said, scooting away from the sleeping child and cracking the window. "Who are you?" she asked.

"Better yet, who are you? And why are you parked on what is obviously private property?"

Joy glanced at her glow-in-the-dark, digital watch. Eleven-thirty. Anger radiated through her body. How dare he? This had to be Gabriel St. John, a man who thought nothing of disappointing a little girl. She'd hoped that he would care for Sophie in a way her mother obviously didn't—that he would treasure her and love her. Joy had hoped this move would be a good one for her little friend, but now she wasn't so sure.

Fueled by the anger pumping through her veins, she popped the lock and opened the door. It was impossible to get a good look at Gabriel St. John, but she didn't need a good look. She needed a shotgun.

"You're going to wake her up," she whispered, beckoning him away from the truck. "And I have a thing or two I'd like to say to you before we do wake her."

The man followed her without saying a word—actually stalked would have been a more appropriate description. Stopping at the porch, Joy turned and faced him. "How dare you? That little girl has been through enough. Living with...well, living with that woman for the last year, and then waiting for you, expecting a huge welcome and finding absolutely nothing. What could have been so important that you weren't here?"

"Who the hell are you, and what are you talking about?"

A moment of doubt cooled her blood slightly. "You are Gabriel St. John, aren't you?"

She could make out his faint nod in the darkness. "And you were expecting Sophie and me, right?"

"Sophie?"

The confusion in that one word said so very much.

"She didn't call, did she? That—" Joy stopped herself. She wanted to strangle Trudi St. John. "Well, I realize you must have seen something in your ex-wife once upon a time, but I can't imagine what. I mean how could she not call you?"

"Sophie's here?"

This time it was Joy who nodded. "She's sleeping in the

truck. We got here about eight, and no one was home. I'm afraid she thinks the worst—that you don't want her any more than her mother does. I told her there must have been some kind of emergency..." Joy's voice trailed off because she was talking to thin air. Gabriel was already at the truck, crawling through the driver's side to reach Sophie.

Joy sat on the edge of the porch, wanting to give father and daughter some privacy for their reunion. She'd only just settled herself when the screaming started.

"Joy? Where's Joy? What have you done with her?"

Joy sprang from the porch and raced to the truck.

"Joy? You didn't leave me, too? Joy?"

She tried to open the passenger door, but it was still locked. Gabriel reached past his daughter's flailing arms and popped the button. Joy reached into the cab, her arms outstretched. They were immediately filled with a sobbing little girl.

"There, there," she comforted. "I would never have left you without saying goodbye. And, goofball, you were still sleeping in my truck. How could I have left?" She laughed, praying the little girl wouldn't notice how forced it was. "Come on, I'll carry you into the house, and we'll get you settled." Though the child was an armful, she scooped her up, trusting Gabriel would follow.

"And then you'll leave?" Sophie asked, her voice hiccupping from her sobs.

Still walking, Joy tightened her hold. "Honey, we've talked about this. I brought you to your dad, and now you'll be with him. I have to get back to my life. Just because I have to go, doesn't mean I don't love you or that I won't miss you. I'll call you, and you'll tell me all about the new and fun things you do..."

She went on describing her phone calls, making up a funny adventure that had to do with a cow and the rodeo clown who rescued her, but all the time she prattled, soothing the child with her voice, she felt her heart breaking. How could a six-year-old have become so firmly entrenched in her heart in such a short time?

Gabriel opened the door and motioned her inside. He flipped

a switch, and the room was flooded with light. More rough-hewn timber formed the walls, and a massive stone fireplace lined the entire east wall. Overstuffed, comfortable-looking furniture and shelf after shelf of books rounded out his decor.

Joy stared at Gabriel, a giant of a man. He hadn't seemed nearly so large outside when her anger was sustaining her. But now, in a well-lit house, he seemed huge. His dark eyes studied her with an intensity that made Joy very uncomfortable.

She set Sophie on the floor and unwrapped the sleeping bag from her tiny frame. "Now, here we are. Why don't you stand here and say a proper hello to your daddy? I'll go back out to the truck and find your overnight bag."

Immediately Sophie wrapped her arms around Joy's leg. "Don't go," Sophie cried, her hysterics beginning all over.

"I'm not going anywhere but to the truck for your pajamas. Why don't you tell your daddy about that truck driver that blew you a kiss?"

The tears slowed, and Sophie's grip loosened. "He blew you the kiss."

Joy shook her head and pasted a smile on her face. "Nope, he blew it to you, and he honked his horn." Joy unwound the arms from her leg and gave Sophie a gentle push towards her father. "Tell him, and I'll go get your stuff. I'll be right back."

She started out the door before either the silent Gabriel or the tearful Sophie could protest. In the comfort of darkness, Joy allowed herself the comfort of a few tears, but by the time she'd reached the truck, she stopped.

She could cry tomorrow. She'd find a hotel, hole up there, and cry her heart out until she purged the pain that had started to radiate through her breast. Maybe the fairies had some special spell to make her go numb. Being so affected was stupid. She'd only known the little girl a couple of days. But she supposed love didn't necessarily follow a clock.

Pulling the neon pink backpack from the jump seat, Joy sniffed back more tears and practiced her smile. She'd get through this. She always did.

"I'm back," she said when she entered the house. She glanced at Gabriel and Sophie. It didn't appear either of them had moved an inch. "How's it going in here?"

"I still don't understand why you're here," Gabriel said.

"Don't go yet," Sophie pleaded, again wrapping herself around Joy's leg.

"Why don't I get this tired little miss to bed, and then we'll discuss why we're here."

Gabriel nodded and started up the stairs to the left of the door. "Her room's up here."

Joy slung the small pack over her shoulder and reached down to pick up the exhausted Sophie. They followed Gabriel up the stairs. A pink spread and ruffled curtains made a stark contrast to the dark wood that apparently covered the walls of the entire house.

"Do you want to help?" Joy asked Gabriel who stood at one side of the door, his hands stuffed into his pockets.

"I think she'd be more comfortable if you helped her." To Sophie he said, "Goodnight, sweetheart. I'm glad you're home." He shut the door softly.

Sophie's eyelids were drooping as, cleaned and pajamaed, she was tucked into her bed. "You're leaving," she whispered as Joy kissed her cheek.

"I'll have to come back tomorrow to unpack all your things from the back of the truck. It's too late tonight. So this isn't goodbye. It's just goodnight."

"I love you," Sophie said.

"And I love you, too." She left Sophie's room and paused on the stairway, reluctant to have Gabriel see her tears.

He had started a fire in the huge fireplace and was sitting in one of the overstuffed wing chairs that flanked it. Obviously a man of few words, he gestured towards its twin. "Now..." he said, his meaning obvious.

"I thought you knew, that your wife—"

"My ex-wife," he corrected.

"I thought your ex-wife, Mrs. St. John, had called you. She's getting married again." Joy watched his face, waiting to see whether his ex-wife's remarriage caused him any pain, but his face gave nothing away. She'd read a description once, *granite expression*, and it certainly applied to Gabriel St. John.

Looking at him, it was obvious where Sophie came by her red hair. His hair was almost a brown, until the firelight hit is just right, then it was a burning auburn.

He was a good-looking man, almost too good looking for Joy's peace of mind. At least six foot, and quite nicely built. Joy sighed. Yes, he was nicely put together.

The small scar above his right eyebrow moved as his brows arched, encouraging her to continue her explanation.

"I was ready to leave this morning when Mrs. St. John asked me to bring Sophie to you. You see, she had decided to elope with William and didn't feel she would have the time to bring Sophie here before she left."

"And Trudi will pick Sophie up after the honeymoon?" Gabriel St. John's expression didn't give a clue as to what he was feeling.

"My understanding is this is permanent. She's given you complete custody of Sophie. I have the papers." Quietly she added, "It seems William doesn't like children."

The first hint of emotion flickered across his face and echoed in his surprised voice. "Trudi thought to have papers drawn up giving me custody?"

Blushing, Joy answered, "Actually, I suggested it might be wise. You know, in case something happens and you can't reach her. She called her attorney, and he faxed them over."

Gabriel sat motionless a moment, and then the stony countenance on his face broke when he smiled. It was a dazzling sight. "I owe you."

"You don't owe me anything," Joy told him, mesmerized by the change in the man. Looking at him caused a fluttering feeling in the pit of her stomach.

"Ah, but I do." That smile again.

"I think I'd best be going. It's late, and I still have to make my way back into town and find a hotel for the night. I'll be back in the morning to unload Sophie's things. We packed up everything: her clothes, her books and more Barbies than I've seen in one room. We brought it all." Joy rose, unsure what else to say. "Could you give me directions to the nearest hotel?"

"You can have the guest room."

Joy shook her head. "Really, that's not necessary. I'd prefer staying at a hotel. I'll be back in the morning."

"Speaking of morning, I was wondering..." Gabriel hesitated.

"Wondering?"

"Since Sophie's arrival was unexpected, I haven't arranged for someone to stay with her while I work. I was wondering if you'd be interested in the job until I do?"

Joy started to respond, but Gabriel kept talking over her. "I'd be willing to match whatever Trudi was paying you and—"

He thought she was an employee of Trudi's. "Mr. St. John..." She planned to tell him she couldn't do it. She had an organization to run and had never been an employee of his ex-wife, but then she thought of the teary-eyed Sophie and found herself saying, instead, "I'd love to stay on and take care of her until you find someone for the job."

"Then you can consider room and board part of your salary, and there will be no more discussion about hotels." He rose from his chair. "Let's go out and get what you need for tonight. We'll unload the rest of Sophie's and your things in the morning."

"All right." Joy's heart was suddenly ten pounds lighter. She wasn't going to have to say goodbye to Sophie tomorrow. Of course, she'd have to explain the real situation to Gabriel in the morning, but she had a reprieve. She followed Gabriel into the star-studded night.

Time. She had more time.

Looking up as a star shot across the sky, Joy made a quiet wish that her reprieve would last a long, long time.

***

"You're still here!" screamed the redheaded whirling dervish who bounced onto Joy's bed. "You're still here, you're still here." Sophie leaned over and grabbed Joy in a stranglehold, squeezing for all she was worth. "I wish you wouldn't leave forever."

Half awake and bleary eyed, Joy reached out and hugged Sophie back. "If wishes were horses everyone would ride. For now, we'll just be happy we have more time." She scooped the child up and slid her under the covers. "Now, what are you doing up so early in the morning?" she asked as she cuddled Sophie close. The digital clock on the nightstand read five-thirty.

"I couldn't sleep. I think there are monsters here," Sophie whispered, snuggling closer.

"Are they big?" Joy asked.

"Yeah."

"Are they hairy?"

"Yeah," Sophie said and yawned.

"Do they smell like oranges?" Joy asked.

"No, like dog poop." A small giggle was interrupted by another yawn.

"Oh, then later today we'll have to find them all and give them a bath, because the only monsters allowed in houses I sleep in are the ones that smell like oranges."

Another tired giggle erupted, muffled by the blankets. "You're silly," Sophie said through another yawn.

"And you're tired, too. Why don't we both go back to sleep for a little while." Five-thirty in the morning was way too early to start the day.

"Can I sleep in here?" Sophie moved even closer, as if she was afraid Joy would somehow escape as she slept.

Joy wrapped her arms around the slight frame. "Sure, as long as you don't snore or hog the covers."

"I won't."

Within minutes the little girl's breathing was even. Holding her close as she closed her own eyes, Joy wondered how she was ever going to let Sophie go. She gave herself a mental shake. She wouldn't think of that now. She'd enjoy the time she'd been granted, and when it was over she'd pick up and go on—just like she always did.

"It's all going to be fine."

Joy jumped. The three fairies stood in a line at the side of the bed.

"You have to stop just popping in on me like that," she whispered, snuggling the sleeping Sophie closer. "You're going to give me a heart attack."

"Sorry." Blossom looked anything but sorry. She looked

excited. "You're staying here?"

"Yes. I know you three have an agenda, and my staying here is going to throw off your time table, but truly, I don't need you to find me a man. I'm happy."

"No, you're not." Fern sat gingerly on the edge of the double bed. "You're going through the motions. You know you want a little girl of your own. Someone like Sophie to hold and love. You know you want a man to love, someone like—"

"Like who we have in mind for you," Myrtle said firmly. She shot a look at Fern, who got off the bed and stood slightly behind her sisters.

Myrtle brushed her hand across Sophie's hair. "You take all the time you need here. The child needs you."

"Thank you. I still don't think I need your help finding Mr. Right," she whispered. But she was whispering to an empty room. The fairies were gone.

Hopefully, they would stay gone until she left the St. John house...or even longer.

***

Gabriel St. John peeked into his daughter's bedroom, but no sleep-tousled head greeted him. His heart skipped a beat, but he calmed himself. Sophie was here, probably downstairs watching cartoons. Gabriel scolded himself for overreacting as he walked down the stairs, but the only thing down there was the early morning sun, shining hazily through the windows.

He looked out the window, suddenly scared Joy and Sophie had disappeared as quickly as they had appeared on his doorstep. Or worse, maybe he'd just imagined the whole thing. Gabriel sighed when he saw Joy's cherry red truck still parked under his pine tree.

He raced back up the stairs and stopped in front of Joy's room. He listened for sounds and, hearing none, cracked the door open. Peeking inside, he heaved a relieved sigh. Sophie's wild red hair flowed over Joy, mingling with the woman's dark brown hair. Entangled under the covers, his baby girl draped across Joy's chest, they slept. Quietly, Gabriel shut the door.

Who was this woman? Sophie obviously cared for her and trusted her a great deal more than she trusted him. That much was obvious. This Joy worked—no she *had* worked—for Trudi. That summed up his knowledge. Joy...he couldn't even recall her last name.

She had long brown hair that framed bright blue eyes and was a little on the short side—he'd put her about five-foot-three—a little too rounded to be fashionable, but she curved in all the right places. He'd noticed that last night. Not that he was looking for a woman, but a man would have to be dead not to look at an attractive woman. And Joy was attractive.

He pushed thoughts of Joy's curves to the back of his mind. Instead he focused on her smile. It's quickness seemed to indicate she used it a lot. It wasn't a business smile, but one that seemed at home on her face, as if she found the world to her liking.

Sophie's Joy looked like a very comfortable woman. Comfortable. That would be a relief. Gabriel St. John had learned to value his comfort and would do anything to maintain it. The four years he'd spent married to Trudi had been anything but. Living hell was the term that generally came to mind when he thought about those times. He'd thought he'd found everything he was looking for. A sleek, stylish woman who would love him, who shared his interests and his goals—a woman he could love.

What he'd gotten was a shallow woman whose only goals or interests centered around her wants and needs. Whatever had passed for love when they first met had soon died. In its place was his love for the daughter they had created together.

Lost in memories, he made his way back down the stairs and poured a cup of coffee. Thinking of Trudi was a painful reminder of what he'd lost. It wasn't losing Trudi that hurt, but the loss of a dream—the dream of a woman he could love and the family they would build. And losing Trudi meant losing that dream, and losing Sophie.

For Sophie he'd stayed and tried to make his relationship with Trudi at least bearable, but in the end it was impossible. When Trudi left, he'd wanted to keep Sophie with him, but he'd lost custody. He'd tried to convince himself that Sophie would be all right, that Trudi needed time to grow into the type of mother Sophie deserved, but...

But. There was always that but. His two months with Sophie in the summer and his Thanksgiving and Easter holidays didn't seem like enough. Every time he saw his daughter, she seemed further away from him, from everyone. When he'd found Sophie in that truck last night, he'd wanted to do nothing more than hug her to him and hold on forever.

He had Sophie back.

The thought was so powerful it seemed surreal.

Joy, the small woman with the big smile, had brought his daughter home to stay. All the time they'd spent apart, all the hurt he thought he saw in Sophie's big brown eyes, all the nights he'd agonized and worried about her, all that was in the past.

Sophie was home.

Maybe it wasn't the family he'd once dreamed of creating, but he and Sophie would build their own family. Now he had his chance. He'd find a way to make up the time they'd lost. He'd find a way to be the type of parent she needed.

He'd find a way, of that Gabriel St. John was sure.

Three

Joy slowly became aware of something tickling her nose, while something else crushed her chest. Sophie.

She forced one of her eyelids open. The world was a blur veiled through the red strands of Sophie's hair. The little girl's body was draped over her, clutching Joy in her sleep as if she feared Joy would disappear while she slept.

Cautiously, Joy disentangled herself, slipped out of bed and checked for fairies. Thankfully, the coast was clear. The clock was flashing a more respectable time now than when Sophie had joined her. Eight-thirty—much later than Joy was accustomed to waking, but understandable. Yesterday had been a long day, both physically and emotionally exhausting. But Joy was refreshed now, ready to go on with her day.

Ready to deal with fairies.

Ready to face Gabriel St. John.

The look on his face last night had convinced her that Sophie would not just be well cared for here, but nurtured. And Gabriel had given her a chance to stay a little longer with Sophie.

The old sweats and t-shirt she used for pajamas were decent enough to be seen in, so Joy walked down the stairs in search of coffee. She mentally began making a list. She'd have to unpack the truck and settle both her things and Sophie's. She'd have to call her family and let them know where she was for now. She'd have to contact Ripples and let the staff know where they could send the papers she needed to look at. She'd have to find someone to take her place at the Carmichaels' party. And then...

Coffee. She'd start working on the list as soon as she had a quart or two of coffee in her. Max yelled at her, saying she was addicted to the brew, but brothers were supposed to worry. Coffee was the magic elixir that started her rolling and kept her moving through her busy days.

As she walked down the stairs, she realized she was too late to start the coffee—at least she was if the delicious aroma wafting up the stairs was any indication.

"Good morning."

She tugged at her t-shirt, making sure she was well covered. "Good morning. If that's coffee I smell, you're going to have my undying gratitude."

He was sitting on the couch, the newspaper lying on his lap, watching her descend the stairs. "Then I guess we're even. I owe you for bringing Sophie home, and you owe me for coffee."

Joy walked into the kitchen and began rooting through cupboards for a mug. Gallon-sized, preferably.

"Left cabinet, over the sink," Gabriel called.

Joy found one—not quite gallon-sized, but it would have to do—and poured her life's blood into the cup. It was a perfect amber color and smelled divine. She took a sip and sighed. "We're definitely more than even. This is the best coffee I've ever tasted, and I've tasted coffee in every state in the union."

"Every?"

"Well, I must confess, I haven't made it to Alaska—yet. I plan to work on that this year."

She walked around the island separating the kitchen from the living room, sank onto the opposite end of the couch and took another appreciative sip.

"Just how is it you've traveled so extensively?" Gabriel asked, his back turned towards his desk as he faced her.

"I...well, you see, I know you assumed I worked for Mrs. St John when I came last night, but I don't."

Gabriel's face froze into the hard mask he'd worn last night. "Then, how did you come to bring Sophie home to me?" His voice had even changed. Gone was the friendly lilt that had accompanied his banter. In its place was a cold barricade that made him unapproachable.

Joy wished she could find some way to batter down those barriers. The urge to reach out and touch him was almost overwhelming. She gripped her coffee mug instead and launched into her explanation. "Well, you see, I was a houseguest of Trudi's and—"

"You're one of her friends?"

She wouldn't have believed it was possible, but his face and voice grew even colder.

Joy took another sip of coffee. "Listen, it generally takes me a cup or two of coffee to get going in the morning, and I seem to be making a bigger mess of things than usual here. Why don't I take this upstairs, drink the entire thing, take my shower and come down and begin my explanation again."

Without waiting for his reply, Joy rose, ready to make her escape. Her foot caught on the edge of a throw rug that was under the coffee table. She stumbled forward, tripped over the coffee table and sprawled. And that was the good news. The bad news—the worst news as far as Joy was concerned—was that she was still holding her coffee mug, and its trajectory hurled it straight at Gabriel St. John.

Even fairy intervention couldn't save her. The coffee landed in his lap and was obviously hot enough to send him flying from the chair. He ripped off his saturated jeans, swearing under his breath as he did it.

"Oh, my God!" Joy cried, scrambling from her ignominious position on top of the coffee table. "What have I done now? Let me get some cold water, so you don't blister." She ran around the island, grabbed the towel and ran cold water over it.

Gabriel was still dancing around as she sprinted back into the living room. "Here," she cried, giving him a little shove back onto the couch. She pressed the cool cloth over his red thigh. "I'm so, so sorry."

The urge to cry was overwhelming. Most of the time she managed to just injure herself or inanimate objects with her clumsiness. Maiming innocent human beings mortified her.

She continued dabbing the cool cloth on his thigh. "I know, I know, you can't wait until I'm gone, and I don't blame you.

I'm such a klutz. But I just want you to know I didn't work for Trudi. I wouldn't have lasted a week. I hate to speak ill of anyone, but your wife—"

"Ex-wife," Gabriel tossed out between gritted teeth.

"Ex-wife is a witch. I was there for money. Oh, not that she paid me a salary or anything. No, I mean that's my job, collecting money. I mean..."

Joy's rapid monologue slowed, and she looked at her hands as if seeing them for the first time. She could feel the twin flames ignite her cheeks as she realized just where her hands had been.

"I'm so sorry," she said again, jerking her hands off his thigh, feeling as if she were the one who'd been burned. "I'll understand if you don't want me to stay with Sophie, and I wouldn't blame you. I—"

A red ball of fire interrupted her as it flung itself across the floor and slammed into Joy. "No! You can't go!"

"Honey," Joy whispered, allowing the child's momentum to push her into a sitting position on the floor. "Honey, you know I have to go."

"No!" she screamed again.

"No," Gabriel said softly. "Our little mishap doesn't change my request. And as for how it came that you were at Trudi's, we'll talk about it later." He rose with more dignity than a man in coffee-splattered boxer shorts should be able to possess, and turned toward the stairs. "Now, I think I'll go clean up. I suggest you two ladies do the same. Then we'll meet back here and try to sort everything out so we'll all be happy."

"I won't let Joy go." Sophie stood, her lips stubbornly set as she glared at her father.

Gabriel sank to his knees in front of Sophie. "And I love you enough not to ask you to let her go for now. Joy will have to get back to her own life sooner or later, but we'll see if we can convince her to make it a little later, okay?"

Sophie looked surprised as she slowly nodded her agreement.

"There. Now, let's all get going. I took today off, but I have to be in the office tomorrow, so we've got a lot to settle and straighten out."

That said, Gabriel St. John stood and walked up the stairs.

"Daddy was in his underwear," Sophie whispered. She started to giggle.

Joy tried not to, but couldn't help herself. She giggled, too. "Yes, he certainly was in his underwear. They were kind of cute, though, don't you think?"

"Not as cute as my fairy princess undies," Sophie assured her quite seriously.

Joy grinned. "Oh, never as cute as fairy princess undies." Fairy princesses made Joy think of her fairy godmothers. Where were they when she needed them? If they had interceded, they could have saved her untold embarrassment and Gabriel third degree burns. Fairy underwear was probably more useful than fairy godmothers, she thought peevishly. "I can't imagine anything could be as cute as your undies."

"Yeah, but his were almost as cute. We can tell him after he comes back down," Sophie suggested.

Joy smothered her giggles. "I don't think that would be wise." A picture of Gabriel's boxer clad body flitted through her mind's eye. He did look more than a little cute. That boxer clad body was one that she was sure to see again in her dreams.

Hot, sweaty dreams.

"No, I don't think it would be wise at all." Joy scooped up Sophie and started up the stairs. "Let's get dressed, and then we'll work this all out."

"Promise?"

"Promise."

***

"Now," Gabriel said. "I think you and I need to get things straightened out."

Sophie was engrossed in a cartoon, and the two adults sat at the breakfast island, sipping new cups of coffee.

"Let's start again. I'm Gabriel St. John. You brought my daughter and custody papers to me. You were at Trudi's getting money, but you don't work for her? A houseguest, but not a friend?"

Joy took a deep breath. "Okay, here goes. I'm Joy Aaronson. Actually, I'm Delphina Joy Aaronson, but with

Delphina for a first name, you can well imagine why I go by Joy."

Gabriel was back to his stony countenance, but his dark eyes looked a little more at ease. "Yes, I guess being a Delphina would be rather burdensome."

"More than that, being a Delphina is pure hell." She was slightly encouraged by his warmer attitude and continued. "I work for Ripples. We're a non-profit organization. We do a little of this and that."

"Ripples?" he murmured, as if it sounded familiar.

"You might have heard of us. We support Squirts, a camp for inner-city kids. And Lily's Pond, a shelter for abused women. We have our fingers in a bunch of other little projects, as well as individual interventions. But all of that takes money and I—"

"You raise it," he supplied.

Joy nodded, pleased they were finally communicating. "Yes. I'm good at it, although it's been getting a little old lately. I've been training a new girl to take over as the fund-raiser. I'm hoping to take a more managerial position in the organization in the future."

"You were a guest at one of Trudi's infamous parties, raising money, and she actually had the nerve to ask you to bring Sophie to me?"

"Well, Sophie and I had hit it off right from the start..." She smiled at the memory. "There was something in her eyes that touched me. I think your ex-wife realized that Sophie and I had connected, and that's why she asked me to bring Sophie here." Realizing she was defending a woman she could barely stomach, Joy shrugged. "She was desperate. She paid for my expenses and wrote a hefty check to Ripples." Her voice softened. "I'm glad she did ask me."

Gabriel smiled. Just like last night, Joy was struck with how just an upturn of his lips changed his entire look. He probably didn't have near enough practice at it, and that was a shame because it was a beautiful sight to behold.

The image of Gabriel wearing only a smile and his boxer shorts flitted unwillingly through her mind and left her feeling flushed. Joy took another fortifying gulp of coffee and tried to put images of Gabriel out of her head. She was here for Sophie.

"I'm glad Trudi asked you as well. But how can you stay, even for the short time it will take me to find someone else to babysit Sophie?"

"Well, I think it's time for Diane, that's my trainee, to solo. I can manage a couple weeks." Joy could only imagine what her family would say about her offering to stay two weeks in the same house with a man she'd just met. She'd always been impulsive, but this was even a bit much for her. She felt nervous, and added, "I mean, if you need me that long."

"I remember where I've heard of Ripples. There was an article in the paper a couple months ago about the organization's interventions that brought a little girl from..."

"Mexico," Joy supplied. "She needed surgery on a cleft lip and palate. It went fine, by the way. She went home to her parents a few weeks ago. Her smile is one of the things that makes my job so worthwhile."

"I seem to recall the article mentioned the founder of Ripples. I didn't pay attention to her name at the time, but I believe it mentioned she started the organization and pretty much still runs things."

Joy was never comfortable with praise. The article, while good for Ripples, had embarrassed her. She tried to laugh it off. "Yeah, she's amazing."

Gabriel gave her a searching look, and slowly a smile blossomed. "Yes, I'm beginning to suspect that she is."

Joy's discomfort increased. She didn't feel as if what she did was all that special, and having people make a fuss over it unnerved her. "So, we're settled? I mean, you want me to stay until you find someone else?"

"Yes. I'd very much like to have you stay. It's obvious Sophie adores you."

Joy thought back to their first meeting. "I think Sophie desperately wanted someone to care, and I just happened to be there."

"And I wasn't there." His voice echoed pain as he said the words, but there was anger on his face. Then he seemed to rein in his emotions. "I'm glad you were there and that you cared. That's a rare thing, Joy. A very rare thing."

Gabriel got up and walked into the kitchen. Joy sat at the table and watched him retreat. His shoulders were stooped, and he wore an aura of sadness.

There was nothing Joy hated more than seeing someone sad. She wanted the people that surrounded her to be happy. It was as simple as that. And sometimes it was as difficult as that.

It looked like she was going to have her work cut out for her with Sophie and Gabriel but, one way or another, Gabriel and Sophie were going to be happy. Whether they liked it or not.

Suddenly Joy thought about the fairies. She hoped they'd take a two-week hiatus before starting their match-making. She had waited almost three decades to find the love of her life. What was two more weeks? She'd just explain things to them. They would understand. After all, they'd said they cared about Sophie.

She went to her room and shut the door. "Myrtle? Fern? Blossom?" She'd never called the fairies before. Would they come?

"Of course we'll come. It's part of the job description."

Fern was the first to appear. She was wearing a forest green chenille robe and sipping a cup of...

"Coffee?" Joy asked.

"Like you, I believe caffeine is the fifth food group."

The other two fairies popped into the room. Blossom wore neon-yellow, fuzzy-footed pajamas. Myrtle was the only one dressed. "Girls," she tsked. Within in the blink of an eye, the other two fairies were dressed as well.

"You called?" Myrtle asked.

"I needed to let you know that your plans will have to wait. You see, I've promised to stay with Sophie until Gabriel can make other arrangements. I just dropped Sophie on him and..." She paused. "I know you have plans, but we'll just have to put them on hold a couple weeks."

"Don't worry," Blossom soothed.

"But, like I said, I'm staying here, not going home to Chicago."

Blossom looked puzzled. "But here is right where we want you."

"Blossom!" Myrtle yelled.

"You mean..." Joy couldn't finish the sentence. She didn't like where she suspected this conversation was going.

"Gabriel," Blossom continued, oblivious to Fern and Myrtle's angry stares. "He needs you. Sophie needs you."

"Gabriel needs me."

"Of course Gabriel."

"But—" Joy stopped. All three fairies were gone. "Cowards. Come back here. This isn't finished."

The room remained empty. Well, if they thought this issue was settled, they were wrong. Wait. The fairies hadn't said Gabriel was the one they were matching her up with. They'd only said he needed her.

Joy felt a surge of what could only be disappointment, but she quickly pushed it aside. She wasn't looking for love, wasn't looking for a happily-ever-after for herself. No, she was looking for happily-ever-afters for Sophie, and now she had the opportunity to find one for her little kindred spirit.

Besides, the idea of Gabriel falling in love with her was laughable. Anyone could see that he wasn't the type of man who would be interested in her. She was too short, too round and too...well, too normal. The Gabriel St. Johns of the world wanted someone more like Trudi. Tall, sleek, stylish and definitely not ordinary.

Maybe the fairies were gone for the duration of her visit. Joy hoped so.

"So, are you staying?"

The door opened, and Sophie ran in full speed. Joy opened her arms as easily as she had opened her heart.

"I'm staying, for a little while," she said as she hugged the child.

"Forever."

Setting Sophie back on the ground, Joy knelt beside her. "Honey, I'm staying for a few days, just until your dad finds someone else. Then I have to go. But, no one can ever take you out of my heart."

"Never?"

"Never."

"Come on, girls, we've got work to do," Gabriel called from the kitchen.

"I'm not a girl, I'm a woman," Joy hollered back as they started down the stairs.

"Oh, no, not one of those mad women libbers?"

"No, just a woman who knows who she is and what she wants," Joy assured him.

"What do you want, Joy?"

Gabriel's question might have been casual, but as Joy looked at Sophie, she felt her heart constrict. She thought of the fairies. They were wrong. No matter how much Sophie meant to her, no matter how quickly Gabriel could raise her blood pressure, it wasn't enough. She might need to be needed, but she wanted something more than that from her happily-ever-after.

Infusing her voice with a lightness she didn't feel, Joy said, "I want to get all this work done so we can play."

"Work it is. I'm always pleased to give my girls what they want."

"Women," Joy and Sophie both said in unison. Joy high-fived the little girl.

Gabriel shook his head. "I can see you've already corrupted my sweet little Sophie."

Joy put thoughts of the fairies and their ridiculous scheme out of her mind as they carried box after box into the house. "How on Earth did you get all this into your truck?" Gabriel grumbled.

Joy looked smug. "I'm a great packer. I've had lots of experience, after all."

Gabriel grunted as he leaned the box against the house and opened the door. "Every state?"

"Except Alaska. And I was thinking there must be some money rattling around up there and waiting for me to scoop it up." Joy propped the door open with her foot and nodded for Gabriel to go in.

"Are those my Barbies?" Sophie cried.

"It's heavy enough that I'm thinking it might be bowling balls." Joy sagged a little under the imaginary weight. "How many did you put in here, anyway?"

Sophie giggled. "I don't have any bowling balls."

"Are you sure? I mean, you seem to have everything else packed in these boxes. I'm sure you must have at least a bowling ball or two." Joy plopped the box onto Sophie's bed.

Sophie shook her head, her twin braids swaying. "Nope."

"Well," Gabriel said, "we'll just have to take care of that. Bowling is quite the American pastime, and everyone one should have their own bowling ball."

"And their own bowling shoes. Wearing someone else's is so gross." Joy held her nose and put on her most disgusted face.

Sophie giggled. "I've never been bowling."

As if Sophie's statement was finally registering, Gabriel made an incredulous face. "You're not serious, are you?" Nervously, Sophie nodded. "You mean, I'm your father, and I've never in your entire life taken you bowling?"

Sophie's head shook even more slowly, and Gabriel's own echoed her motion. "I should be forced to eat pizza once a week for the next month."

Joining in the spirit of things, Joy tried to look stern. "Starting tonight, right?"

Seriously, Gabriel nodded. "Tonight. And of course we'll have to get it with lots of cheese and pepperoni, which are Sophie's favorites. I'll just have to torture myself by accepting it."

"And of course you hate cheese and pepperoni?" Joy asked. The stony man she'd met yesterday had disappeared. In his place was a laughing, fun-loving man—a man Joy suspected she could easily like. Very, very easily. Thinking of the fairies, she mentally added, *but nothing more than like.* He needed her. That's what they said. He just needed her until he could find someone else to care for Sophie.

Gabriel looked at Joy in mock horror. "Oh, gross. Please, don't make me eat it. I'll take you bowling this week. I'll even buy you your own shoes, but just don't make me eat pepperoni."

"What do you say, Sophie?" The little girl looked unsure. "Come here, I'll tell you what." Joy leaned down and whispered into Sophie's ear. When they straightened, she looked very seriously at Gabriel. "We've decided pizza once a week for a month isn't enough."

"No?" Gabriel asked.

"No. We've decided that you need..."

Joy and Sophie both roared, "A tickle party."

"Get him," Joy shouted. She watched as Sophie attacked with all the verve of a six-year-old.

Gabriel put up a valiant fight, but in the end he was reduced to teary laughter.

"I won," Sophie yelled.

"Yeah, you showed him. I bet he'll never dare not teach you how to bowl again."

"Never," Gabriel swore, raising his hand to seal the vow. "But, I think people who instigate fights should be prepared to suffer the consequences."

"You wouldn't," Joy said, edging her way off the bed.

"Would, too."

She took a step toward the door. "We've only just met. My brothers at least gave me a few years to get to know them before they started torturing me."

"Ah, those were brothers, I'm a..." he groped for a word.

"Friend?" Joy supplied as she sprinted out the door. She raced down the stairs with Sophie and Gabriel hot on her trail. She stopped on the far end of the couch.

Circling warily, she said, "Sophie, you're supposed to be my kindred spirit. Why are you helping your non-bowling father capture me?"

"'Cause it's your turn," Sophie said, an evil twinkle in her eye.

Sophie was going to be fine here. Joy was sure of it. She smiled at the thought and played along with the game. "My turn for what?"

"Time for tickles," Sophie screeched. She broke for the left, Gabriel broke for the right, and they both cornered Joy.

"I'm allergic to tickles," Joy protested as she let Sophie

tackle her.

"You can't be allergic to tickles," Sophie said and dug in.

"Help!" Joy shrieked. "Gabriel, don't just stand there, get this wicked monster off me."

Instead of helping Joy escape, he pinned her feet to the ground.

"I'm a guest," she protested to no avail.

Sophie tickled mercilessly, and finally Joy said, "Okay, uncle! You win, I lose. You're the champ of tickles."

"I win, and we get pizza," Sophie hollered and jumped off Joy's battered frame.

"You can let go of my legs now," Joy said as she tried to raise herself into a sitting position. Gabriel leaned towards her as she finished sitting up, and their heads cracked. "Ow," Joy squealed. She began to rub the offended spot.

"Let me look," Gabriel said, reaching for her head with his left hand even as his right massaged his own injured skull.

"Kiss it, Daddy. Make it better like you make my boo-boos better," Sophie prompted.

"Would you like a kiss, Joy?" Gabriel asked.

Her heart kicked into hyper-drive. "Kiss?"

His hand pushed hers aside as he massaged the small bump. "Would you like me to kiss your boo-boo like I kiss Sophie's?"

"I don't think I need a kiss." Joy's voice sounded foreign to her ears. What she wanted to say was, *Oh, yes, I'd like you to start at my boo-boo and work your way down to—*

The front door flew open, interrupting Joy's lusty thoughts. A beautiful woman stood there scowling at the scene.

"Joy, help! It's the wicked witch," Sophie squealed and ran for her lap.

Gabriel's hand froze in Joy's hair. "Helen," he said.

Four

Joy gave Gabriel a little shove, trying to remind him that he was practically sitting on her with one hand still resting in her hair.

"Gabriel, what's going on here? You said you were taking a sick day. I came here to nurse you back to health. What are you doing with this woman and kid?" Helen's voice didn't raise a decibel, but her annoyance was as readily apparent as if she'd been yelling.

Joy was used to dealing with all types of people. It was her job, after all. Some she liked, and some she loved. Very few did she actively dislike.

Helen moved to the top of that very short list.

"I know this doesn't look very good," Joy said, more to help Gabriel, who wasn't saying anything, than to offer up an explanation.

"Gabriel?" Helen had obviously decided that Joy was to be ignored.

In a voice colder than any Joy had ever heard from him, he said, "Helen, this *kid* happens to be Sophie, my daughter. And the woman is Joy. I'm sure she'd appreciate being addressed as such. She's a friend who has graciously agreed to put her own life on hold to give me a hand getting Sophie settled."

Sophie's *wicked witch* did an about face. A smile appeared on her lips, but it didn't quite reach her eyes. "Oh, so this is Sophie." She walked toward the child, who still clung to Joy,

nd from her imposing height said, "I've heard so much about you. I hope you and I can learn to be friends during your visit."
"Sophie's not just here for a visit. She's here to stay permanently," Gabriel said. "And I have Joy to thank for that."
Joy rose, Sophie still clinging to her. Even standing she still she had to look up at Helen—way up. At five-three, Joy was accustomed to craning her neck when talking to people, but she would have rather met Helen-the-Amazon face to face.
"Yes, Sophie's here to stay, so you'll have plenty of time to get to know her."
"Oh, isn't that wonderful," Helen said. Her smile grew broader, but her eyes seemed to grow even harder. "So you're not sick?"
When Gabriel shook his head, Helen looked almost disappointed. "I thought I'd spend the day nursing you back to health, but since that obviously isn't going to be necessary, I think it's time for me to leave. I can't just walk away from my work whenever the whim strikes me." She gave Joy a meaningful look.
Gabriel took her by the elbow and walked her towards the door. "Thank you so much for coming. I know we have a lot to discuss—"
"We can do that at dinner Saturday night." She stopped and looked at him. "We are still on for dinner, aren't we?"
The last thing Joy heard as they walked through the door was Gabriel saying, "Of course."
"She's a wicked witch, I just know it," Sophie whispered after Gabriel had shut the door.
Though Joy was inclined to agree, she sensed that this particular witch was going to be a part of Sophie's new life. That she had come to nurse Gabriel back to health and that they were going out Saturday night indicated more than a casual relationship. "Helen isn't a witch. She's someone who is obviously important to your father, and I'm sure when you get to know her you'll like her." *Yeah, when pigs fly,* she thought, but held her tongue.
"No, I won't like her." Sophie sounded sure of herself.
"Why don't you just give her some time?" Joy soothed.

"And it seems to me we've got some boxes to unpack."

"Okay, but I'm not going to like her."

This could be trouble, Joy thought. But she couldn't think of a way to avoid it.

***

Later that afternoon, Gabriel had, after a great deal of fast talking, convinced Sophie to accompany him to the store. Sophie still wasn't quite ready to trust her father, but she'd regain that trust in time. Gabriel loved her. If Joy could see it, eventually Sophie would, too.

While they were gone, Joy decided to make the phone calls she'd been putting off. The call to Ripples was easy enough. But she was sure the call to Max wouldn't go as smoothly.

She dialed the number. "Hello?" answered a definitely feminine voice.

Granted a reprieve, Joy smiled and greeted her sister-in-law. "Grace, and how is our beautiful little Charity?"

"Joy? CheChe is doing fine. Actually, if I had one-tenth her energy level, I'd...well, I'd get a heck of a lot more done." Grace's rich laughter floated over the wire. "Max told me you met The Girls."

"Your fairy godmothers? Maybe you can explain it better than Max did." A part of her still wanted to have someone tell her that the fairies were just some big joke.

"I'm not sure I understand it myself. I thought I was crazy, and that's how I met Max."

Joy couldn't imagine her brother accepting the existence of fairies without proof. "And Max didn't have you committed?"

"I think he wanted to believe me right from the start. There was this...oh, I don't know how to explain it. But there was something. He didn't dismiss the fairies, or me, right out of hand. And after a time, he came to believe in them as well." Her voice dropped. "You're not crazy. Or, if you are, then Max and I are, too."

"I'm not sure if I feel relieved or not."

"Do you know who it is they have their eye on?"

"I really didn't call about the fairies," Joy answered. She might have thought they hinted about Gabriel being the one, but she'd obviously been mistaken. Gabriel needed her. That's what they had said. Obviously, he just needed her to stay with Sophie, and that's why the fairies were content to let her stay here for two weeks.

For himself Gabriel needed someone classy. Someone like Trudi, or Helen. There was no room in his life for someone like Joy. The thought was strangely disheartening, and Joy changed the subject. "I was calling to tell Max it looks like I might be in the area for a while, and I was hoping to get over to visit you."

"How close?" Grace asked.

"Actually, in Greene Township." Just on the outskirts of Erie, Gabriel's house was only about a half hour from Max's. "I'm helping a friend out for a couple weeks."

"What friend?" Grace asked. "Never mind. I sound like I'm cross-examining a witness. Maybe I should ask Nick for a job? Max says one of these days my curiosity will get the best of me."

"Oh, I've heard Max say a couple other things about you," Joy teased. "I'm just staying here for a few weeks to help Gabriel—"

"*Gabriel?*"

Joy cringed. She should have known Grace would pounce on a name.

"He's just someone I'm helping out. Helping is what I do—it's what Ripples does." There. Let Grace think Joy was here working for Ripples. "Plus, Gabriel's seeing someone, so I'm sure he's not the one."

Suddenly, Joy was surrounded by fairy godmothers. "Darn," she muttered as she nervously eyed the colorful trio.

"Oh, yes, Gabriel's the one," Blossom said merrily. "When we said he needed you, we meant it. He needs you in his life. He's the one."

Joy covered the receiver and hissed, "He's not."

"I think you're definitely protesting too much," Fern chuckled.

"But Gabriel's not married, is he?" Grace asked over the phone line.

Joy glared at the grinning fairies. "No, actually he's

divorced, and he's currently involved with a lovely woman named Helen." She crossed her fingers behind her back and said a silent prayer for forgiveness. Lovely and Helen were two words that didn't belong in the same sentence.

Blossom must have thought so, too, because she snorted.

Carrying on a five-way conversation was too much for Joy in her befuddled state. "Really, he's not the one. I don't think there is one. Listen, I've got to run. I'll try to make it over this weekend. Tell Max I'll talk to him. Bye." She hung up quickly and faced the fairies. Tweedle Dee, Tweedle Dum and Tweedle Dumber.

"Hey," Blossom shouted. "That wasn't nice."

"Eavesdropping on my thoughts as well as my phone conversations?"

"You've read the books. You know we can sense our godchildren's thoughts. So, I wasn't really eavesdropping. And, you're a loud thinker."

Since Joy couldn't argue about how loud her thoughts were, she simply continued her offensive. "If you're going to listen, you can't expect to hear good things. I thought you all were going to give me a break until I'm done here?"

"No, you didn't. We told you that Gabriel's the man for you, and that means you need us to help."

"No, you said he needed me. I assumed you meant he needed me to take care of Sophie. And, he's got Helen." A woman who could model for any fashion magazine. "So, I don't need you."

"He doesn't have Helen for long." The expression on Fern's face made Joy feel a momentary stab of pity for Helen.

"You wouldn't hurt her, would you?"

"I can see we need to clear up a few rules." Myrtle was suddenly all business. "We don't hurt anyone, not ever. It's one of the first fairy laws. And Gabriel can't see us. You can tell him about us if you want, but that doesn't necessarily mean he'll believe in us."

"He'd think I was crazy." Which wasn't much of a stretch. Joy herself thought she was crazy, despite Max and Grace's reassurances.

Fern smiled. "You're luckier than Gracey was. You have two people assuring you that you're not crazy."

"Plus the three of us. We'd tell you if you were nuts."

Somehow, mind-reading fairies reassuring her of her sanity didn't make Joy feel better. "If I'm not nuts now, with the three of you popping in on me all the time, it shouldn't take me long to get there."

"Now, Joy." Myrtle wagged a finger at her, like some neon-haired teacher. "We're only trying to help."

"I don't need your help." She was a simple woman who lived a simple life. At least life had been simple until she met three fairies.

"Yes, you do. You want someone to love." Blossom looked as if she was going to swoon in a very Scarlet O'Hara sort of way.

Thoughts of fairy matchmaking didn't make Joy want to swoon. It made her quake with fear. Her doubt in their abilities must have shown in her eyes, or they were eavesdropping again, because Fern laughed. "Oh, yes you need us. More than you've ever realized."

"Please. Why don't you three take a vacation. I'll call you when I need you." They'd be waiting a long time for that particular phone call to come through.

"You need us now." Myrtle obviously wasn't buying Joy's ploy. "If you didn't, we wouldn't be here."

"Now about this Helen," Blossom said. "She's our biggest hurdle to date. We've been thinking maybe a disease—"

"No way," Joy warned.

"Joy." Exasperation tinged Myrtle's voice. "Remember we can read your mind, and we'd never do anything that would really harm her. Just a nice little illness that would keep her out of the way while Gabriel realizes he loves you."

"But I don't love him."

"You love Sophie." Fern seemed determined to see this thing through.

"That's not enough of a reason to fall in love with her dad."

"You love watching him with her." Blossom's voice was more sing-songy than usual. "You love seeing him smile."

"And his boxer shorts," Fern added. "Don't forget the boxer shorts."

Joy couldn't deny it, but it still wasn't enough. She wanted what Grace and Max had, what her mother and father had. She wasn't settling for less.

"And we're here to give you that." Myrtle smiled. "With Gabriel."

"Listen, you do whatever you want, but Gabriel's never going to love me. And, if you have fairy rules, then I think it's time I put down some goddaughter rules. First and foremost, you may not do anything to Helen. No illnesses, no kidnappings, no broken bones..." She searched him mind for some of the fairies' other tricks in Grace's books. "No deserted islands. Nothing. Leave her alone."

"Spoilsport." Fern looked disappointed. "I was thinking of a mysterious rash that turned her face green. I'm rather fond of green."

"I was voting for yellow," Blossom added merrily.

"No rashes, no matter what color. No diseases."

When Fern and Blossom started to object, Myrtle raised her hand, silencing their objections. "No diseases. As a matter of fact, we promise to leave Helen alone."

"And Gabriel? You won't cast some spell to make him think he loves me?"

"Honey," Myrtle patted Joy's hand reassuringly, only Joy wasn't reassured. "There are many things we can do, but love is a magical process not even we can influence. So, put your mind at ease."

"I don't think my mind will be at ease until this is over."

"Then we'd better get you and Gabriel together as soon as possible."

With that the three fairies blinked out of the room.

Joy decided their visit had only made her more nervous. If they weren't going to mess with Helen, just what did the fairies have in mind?

***

"'...Please, tell me, where is my dearest Beast?' Beauty begged." Joy paused and looked at the sleeping little girl curled so comfortably against her. Sophie's red hair, released from its braids, fanned over her pillow in little waves. Joy stroked a strand and gently kissed Sophie's forehead.

That Sophie had crept so rapidly into her heart, taking up so much room, amazed her. It was like fairy magic, only the fairies said love was more magic than they could handle. Maybe Sophie had touched her so fast because she reminded Joy of herself at that age. Oh, outwardly there was no resemblance, but the girl had seemed so lost in her mother's house. Joy remembered how that felt.

She'd grown up the younger sister of two phenomenal brothers. Max and Nick had always seemed so at ease with themselves, so sure of where they were going. With Joy, nothing had come as easily. She'd been an awkward child who physically developed long before her peers. She had curves and padding when the ideal female body was emaciated and straight. She'd been an average student who enjoyed quiet evenings at home more than wild party scenes.

Max had gone into psychiatry, prying into people's psyches. Nick was an attorney, champion of the underdog. For years Joy had wandered, not sure what sort of job would fulfill her. It wasn't a job that required college—one term of classes had been enough to convince her of that.

Her family wasn't rich, but they could all live comfortably for the rest of their lives without working a day. Thanks to her grandmother, Joy's personal trust was large enough that work wasn't a priority. But she'd knownliving as a lady of leisure wasn't what she wanted, either. Then one day she found out an acquaintance had been abused for years by a spouse and that the woman had nowhere to escape. That's when the idea for Ripples was born and became Joy's passion.

The first Lily's Pond had opened, providing a place for women to go and be safe. A place where they could heal. And from there, Joy had found her calling. She'd had no desire for some high-powered career, but she did know people and genuinely liked them. And, in addition to helping others, she'd discovered that she had a knack for relieving people of their money to support her cause.

What had started as a local foundation was now a national one. The fairies were wrong. Joy didn't need anything else. Running Ripples was enough to fulfill five people's lives.

She stroked Sophie's hair one last time. No, she didn't need anything, but that didn't stop her from occasionally dreaming of having a child to love. And Gabriel...She shut off the thought.

Scooting off the bed without jiggling it, she quietly left the room. She could hear the television and padded down the stairs. Gabriel was on the couch, his feet propped against the coffee table and papers propped against his thighs.

"Am I intruding?" Joy asked.

He put the papers down, clicked off the TV with the remote, and patted the space on the couch next to him. "Not at all. Actually, you can save me from myself. I'm trying to go over some figures, and they're all starting to run together."

Joy felt strangely reluctant to sit so close to Gabriel. Thoughts of fairy match-makers, boxer shorts and the way his hand had felt in her hair—the way her heart had sped when Sophie started begging him to kiss her... She gave herself a mental shake. No, the more distance she put between herself and Gabriel St. John, the better. She ignored the spot on the couch and sank into the chair across from him.

"It's so quiet out here. Most of the time, my work takes me to cities. I'd forgotten how quiet it can be in the country."

"I think I've got the best of both worlds here. We're only twenty minutes from downtown Erie, and I still have crickets singing in my backyard during the summer." He took off his glasses and rubbed his brow.

It was the first time Joy had seen his glasses, and she thought they added a look of distinction to his already near-perfect image.

Gabriel placed the glasses on the pile of paperwork. "I need time away from the city to truly be away from work and the whole rat race."

"Well, I can see why you like it here."

"Tell me more about what you do," Gabriel prompted.

"I'm pretty sure it's your turn to tell me a story. You already know a little about what I do, and I know nothing about what you do."

"I own a small company. We manufacture a new line of motherboards." At her blank look he added, "For computers." He talked of motherboards and circuitry and other terms that meant little to Joy. She didn't interrupt, didn't want to. Instead, she listened to the steady rhythm of his voice and watched his face. Some new circuit he was developing as a prototype caused his entire face to light up. Words like *innovative* and *growth potential* tripped from his tongue as his eyes echoed the thrill she heard in his voice.

She didn't need to be a computer expert to sense his excitement and sense of accomplishment. Despite her lack of computer experience, she found herself becoming excited on his behalf. "That's wonderful!"

Suddenly, Gabriel stopped. His eyes narrowed as he studied her. "You didn't understand a single thing I was talking about, did you?"

Joy chuckled. "Well, I have heard of circuits, of course, and I did realize that everything had to do with computers. But past that...No."

"I'm sorry. Trudi always got so frustrated when I would go on and on."

Joy stopped him. "Please don't apologize. I enjoyed listening to you. I'm sure that, though I didn't understand much of what you were talking about, I could learn if you wanted to explain some of the technical terms to me."

"Really, I don't want to bore you with computer terms you have no interest in."

"Gabriel, I have a brother who is a psychiatrist. I've learned a lot about bi-polar personalities and manic depressives. And Nick's an attorney, so I know about briefs and dockets. Then there's my sister-in-law. She writes, so I know about book tours and agents..." She stopped. "Do you get the picture? I don't mind learning. I mean, while I'm here, I bet I can bend your ear about the joys and woes of Ripples. Or how to twist an arm, empty a pocket, and do it with a big enough smile that the person you're twisting really doesn't mind."

Gabriel chuckled. "You're a different kind of lady, Joy

Aaronson."

"So I've been told on more than one occasion. Now, I know you clicked off the television, but I was hoping you wouldn't mind leaving it on. I thought I heard the theme song for *Friends*, and it just so happens I have a thing for Chandler."

"I guess I might have a tiny little thing for Phoebe," he admitted.

"Phoebe? I thought you'd be the Rachel type."

"And I thought you'd go for Joey, so where does that leave us?"

"With Ross and Monica?" She laughed. "Just turn the TV on."

"Bossy." The word sounded like a caress, and for a moment, Joy forgot she wasn't interested in Gabriel St. John. For one brief moment, she could almost imagine what it would be like to have him whisper a real endearment. *Darling. Sweetheart.* He'd have his hand in her hair again, but this time he wouldn't be rubbing a bump. No, he'd be caressing her, calling her darling, kissing her...

No. That was enough of those kind of thoughts. She wasn't interested in Gabriel St. John. And it wouldn't do to have her mind-reading, nosy fairy godmothers hear these particular inner thoughts.

She jerked from her momentary daydream when Gabriel repeated, "You're a very bossy woman." He picked up the remote control and turned on the television.

Joy forced a laugh. "Gabriel, you ain't seen nothin' yet."

They sat back and enjoyed the half hour of fun and laughter. There was nothing forced about it. For thirty glorious minutes, Joy forgot that she was haunted by fairies and daydreaming about a man who, despite what the fairies said, would never see her as more than a caretaker for his daughter.

"You know, I can't remember the last time I just sat back and enjoyed watching a show with a woman." Gabriel's expression was puzzled.

"Well, I don't know about the women you hang with, but where I come from it's considered pretty normal to have a favorite TV show. We even eat dinner, sometimes just nuking something out of the freezer. We wake up with our hair a mess and no make-up on and..." Her voice dropped to a whisper, "...sometimes we even use the bathroom."

"Do tell," Gabriel said, easily falling into her banter.

"Honest and truly. Why, just last year my mom went out to a restaurant and excused herself to use the bathroom, and she didn't even powder her nose."

"And they allowed that?" Gabriel mimicked a look of shock.

Joy was unable to keep up the absurdity. "I think I'm getting a bit too punchy. These last few days have been busy. It might be early, but it's time to say goodnight." She stood. "Goodnight, Gabriel. I can't remember the last time I was just able to sit and relax. I've been fund-raising for months, and the type of people I've been hanging with aren't the type to sit and watch *Friends* on a Thursday night."

"I imagine they're the type to sip their port and smoke cigars?"

"Oh, my gosh, you know them?" she asked, batting her eyes innocently.

He chuckled and shook his finger in her direction. "You're right, you need to get some sleep. Go to bed."

Bed. Gabriel. It would be a heck of a lot more fun than going to sleep in a solitary sort of way, not that she was interested, she silently amended, in case the fairies were listening. "Gabriel, you're definitely not what I expected."

Gabriel rose. "And you, Joy Aaronson, aren't what I would have expected, if I had been expecting you at all."

Joy took the first couple stairs. "I think it's a good thing you weren't expecting me. You might have run off in fear."

Gabriel grabbed her shoulder and spun her around. "No, I don't think that would have happened. Not at all."

He was going to kiss her. Joy could see it in his eyes. She should pull away, but she didn't move as his lips came closer, closer, and then moved upwards. Gently he kissed her forehead. "You're something else, Joy, something else altogether."

Joy pushed aside the brief feeling of disappointment and strove to capture the same light-hearted tone they'd used all night. "Ah, Gabriel, you've just summed up the story of my life."

Flustered, she backed up a step. "Good night," she whispered and fled up the stairs. At the top, she missed a step and stumbled, but this time she didn't fall. Maybe the fairies were really looking out for her. She thanked them silently as she ran to her room and shut the door.

Safely inside with a closed door separating her and Gabriel St. John, Joy held a hand to her chest. Her heart was pounding hard enough that she worried it was going to explode.

No, Gabriel St. John wasn't what she'd expected at all. But one platonic kiss on the forehead wasn't going to make her fall for a man who was already spoken for.

"Not enough?" Myrtle asked.

Joy spun around, ready for another round with her unwanted godmothers, but the room was empty.

"Cowards," Joy whispered. "I'm not going to fall in love with Gabriel, no matter what."

But even as she spoke the words, Joy worried that it was already too late. Gabriel St. John would be an easy man to love. The tenderness he used with Sophie, the laughter and easy banter, the gentleness she sensed in the big man. Yes, he'd be an easy man to love. And every minute she spent with him was another chip at the armor she was desperately trying to build around her heart.

Five

"Sophie?" Gabriel called.

Thank God it was Friday. Gabriel loved his job, but today he'd wanted to delegate all his work and rush home—home to Sophie and Joy. It had been a long time since he'd had anyone to hurry home to.

"Sophie," he called again, shutting the front door. Gabriel heard Sophie's smothered giggle and sensed a game was afoot.

"Joy?"

"Ready, set..." Joy whispered. "Go." The two of them bounded from behind the kitchen's island and yelled, "Boo."

Gabriel rocked backwards in mock horror and gave what he thought was a very convincing shriek. "You two scared me," he accused, much to Sophie's delight.

She ran up to him. "Joy's teaching me how to fight dirty. She says when someone's bigger than you, you have to use every..."

"Advantage," Joy supplied.

"Yeah, advantage." Sophie accepted his quick hug and continued talking as if nothing special had happened. It was the most contact she'd allowed her father since they arrived, but to Gabriel it was more than special. He watched Sophie, the wonder of her being here—being home—still fresh and overwhelming.

"Joy's brothers were both bigger than her," Sophie continued, "so she used to think of ways to get them. Once, she went into their room real early in the morning. She screamed, 'The bus is coming' and they both jumped out of bed and started to get dressed. Then she started to giggle 'cause it was only—"

"Saturday." Joy giggled.

Gabriel couldn't help chuckling as well. Joy's sense of humor, her sense of life, was contagious. Since she'd walked into his life, Gabriel found himself marveling at how appropriate her name seemed.

"Saturday," Sophie repeated. "They made her pay 'cause they're boys, and boys always make you pay."

"How did they make you pay?" Gabriel asked, looking at Joy with interest.

"I don't think that now would be the time to talk about it because I can see the desire for revenge in your eyes."

"Maybe it's not revenge I'm desiring," Gabriel murmured.

No, not revenge. That kiss last night—that one chaste kiss on the forehead—had left him wondering what really kissing Joy would be like.

The fantasy was broken when Sophie cried, "I know what they did Daddy."

Pulling his attention from his fantasies, Gabriel watched in delight as Joy stuck out her tongue.

"Traitor," she snarled at Sophie.

Gabriel wrapped his arms around his giggling daughter. "Sophie's not a traitor. She's a smart girl who has decided giving up a comrade is preferable to being tortured herself."

"It's okay. You go on and tell him, Miss Sophie St. John. Just remember, I fight dirty." Joy gave the child the evil eye.

"I didn't say anything," Sophie shouted as she ran up the stairs, laughing.

"No fair threatening a little girl to save yourself." Gabriel rose and watched as Sophie ran up to her room. She was home. How many times would he think that thought until the idea felt real?

"I never claimed to fight fair. As I told Sophie, I fight dirty." Joy started towards the kitchen. "Have you made any progress with finding someone to stay with Sophie while you work?"

She didn't look at him, but gave her full attention to the sauce that was bubbling merrily on the stove. Gabriel had the feeling she was uncomfortable, though he wasn't sure why. She'd seemed comfortable enough last night, at least until he kissed her. But it was just a peck on the forehead. It didn't mean anything.

So why had that one small kiss been a prominent feature in his dreams last night? Why had it kept creeping into his thoughts all day?

Without thinking, he moved closer to her. Her soft floral scent was enticing. "Since it's Friday, I thought I'd start looking next week. I can't imagine I'd make much headway over the weekend."

Joy picked up the wooden spoon and stirred the sauce with a clockwise motion.

"I imagine you're right," she said. "Monday then. Are you planning to look at daycare centers or have someone come in?"

"I hadn't given it much thought."

"Well, there are pluses to both options. In a daycare center, Sophie would have the opportunity to mingle with other kids her age. I don't think there was much of that at your wife's, uh, ex-wife's house. But, with everything else that's going on in her life, I'm not sure it's the way to go, despite the kids. I mean, it might be wise to let her spend these last few weeks of summer vacation getting reaccustomed to her surroundings. That way, when school starts, she might be ready for another big change."

"Well, I—"

"I know, it's hard to decide which way to go," she continued as if he hadn't spoken. "But she'll be meeting all kinds of kids in school. She's bound to make friends right away."

She slowly brought the spoon to her lips and blew on it before tasting the sauce. Gabriel's mouth went dry and his body tightened. Only a sick, sick man got excited by a woman cooking. She was just tasting sauce. What was the matter with him?

Joy seemed oblivious to his reaction. She reached for the oregano and sprinkled liberally. "And have you thought about where she'll go to school? I mean, what kind of education does your school district offer? Would you be better off placing her at some private school in town, close to your office? That way when there are school activities during the day you might have a better chance of sneaking out to go to them. I—"

Gabriel reached from behind her and he gently placed his hands over her own. Guiding her, he placed the spoon on the rest and turned her around. "Do you ever let a man get a word in?"

"I'm sorry. Feeling the need to take over and manage things is a terrible habit of mine. I'm sure whatever decision you make will be the right one."

"Really, I don't mind. It's interesting to see how your mind works. But I have to ask, why do you care so much, Joy? Why are you here?" She turned her head away, trying to get back to the sauce, but Gabriel held her in place. He cupped her chin in his hand and turned her face back towards his. "Why?"

That was the question he kept coming back to. But he wanted to know more than why she cared so much about his daughter. He wanted to know why she was affecting him—and she definitely was affecting him.

"Joy?" Gabriel prompted. His fingers trailed across her cheek as he reluctantly released her.

"I don't know," she said softly. "I've been wondering myself. I've spent the last five years traveling. I've met scads of kids, but not one has ever taken up a corner of my heart like Sophie. Maybe it was because she reminded me so much of myself at her age. Or maybe it is just that—like I told her—we're kindred spirits, and we just recognized each other. All I know is Sophie matters to me. She matters enough that I'll juggle my schedule for a couple weeks, or longer if necessary."

Gabriel wanted her to say more, wanted to hear Joy say that she was staying because of him as well. That he mattered. But that was absurd. They'd just met. How could he matter to her? A better question might be, why did Joy matter to him? Was it just gratitude? Were these strange feelings simply a sense of thankfulness that she'd brought his daughter home? Gabriel didn't think so, but he wasn't ready to think about what else those feelings could represent.

"I mean," she continued, "there's no one I have to answer to, not even at work. I make my schedule, so I can juggle it at will."

"In case I haven't said it, thank you," Gabriel whispered. For half a moment he thought about kissing her again and wondered how she'd respond. But the moment passed, and Gabriel released her.

Striving to recapture their easy comradery of last night, he asked, "Now, do I get a taste of this sauce? The smell has been driving me crazy with desire since I walked in the door."

Of course it's the sauce he desires, Joy thought. For a moment she'd thought there was something in his eyes, something more than just an appreciation of her cooking skills, but obviously she was wrong.

With fascination she watched him take the spoon from its rest and dip it into the bubbling red liquid. He brought it to his lips and held it there, savoring it. "Mm," was his only comment as he took a tiny portion off it. "Honey, we could market this and make a fortune."

He was just tasting sauce, not tasting her. But, God, she'd love to have him sipping every inch of her, then she'd reciprocate and they'd...

Joy cut off the fantasy. She had to stop having these strange flights of fancy that seemed to attack her whenever Gabriel was in the vicinity. She shouldn't allow herself to even secretly fantasize about him. The fairies would catch wind of those daydreams, and then there would be trouble.

She concentrated on the fact that Gabriel was just a man. She was only here with him because he was Sophie's father.

"We might make a fortune selling the sauce, but my great-grandmother would come and haunt us both. It's an old family recipe."

"A secret recipe?" Gabriel asked.

"Sometimes things are better left a secret." Secrets. Joy suddenly had a number of secrets in her life. Secret fantasies and three fairies— airy godmothers—were quite a secret. But even more secret were the feelings that Gabriel seemed to be awakening—feelings totally separate from what she felt for Sophie. Feelings that were best left unidentified.

"And sometimes things need to be shared to be appreciated,"

Gabriel said, still talking about the sauce, she was sure.

She only wished she'd been speaking of it as well. *Pull yourself together*, she reprimanded herself. All she was feeling was a good old-fashioned case of lust. Gabriel was easy on the eyes, and it had been a long time since Joy had been in the company of a male for more than a day or two. But Gabriel was spoken for, and Joy had a life to get back to. And that, thankfully, was that. Joy didn't need any complications in her life, and lusting after Gabriel St. John would be a huge complication.

"About the sauce—don't hold your breath on this one. My family would disown me if I shared the recipe." Nervously, she moved to the refrigerator and took out a head of lettuce. "And, speaking of family, my brother Max lives just outside Erie. I don't know what you normally do on Saturdays, but if you're not going into the office, I thought I might go and spend the day with them tomorrow. It would give you and Sophie a chance to be alone and get used to relying on one another. Would that be a problem?"

"Would you be back in time to stay with Sophie while I go to that business dinner with Helen tomorrow night? If not, I can back out. She'll understand that things are a bit unsettled with Sophie's unexpected arrival."

Remembering the Helen that had stormed the house breathing flames, Joy doubted she was the understanding type. "I'll wait and go in the afternoon and take Sophie with me, then there's no worry."

"Joy, I've already let you put yourself out too much and—"

"I'd prefer you thought of this as the first decent vacation I've had in years. I love to cook, and I haven't had much of an opportunity to indulge myself. I've got dozens of books I want to read that I never quite manage to get to and Alice, the wonder who holds Ripples together, is sending me a lot of the paperwork I've fallen behind on."

"But—"

She ignored what she thought might be a protest and continued, "I have my laptop and will probably be getting more paperwork done here than I have in years. So, don't feel guilty about letting me indulge myself." Her voice dropped, "And spending an afternoon with Sophie is indulging myself. She's quite a kid."

"Yes, she certainly is, but it takes quite a woman to recognize that."

"Oh, I don't know about that." Joy turned back to the sauce, suddenly feeling flustered. Everything about Gabriel was flustering her tonight, and she wasn't sure why. "Speaking of Sophie, why don't you go find her and get her washed up for dinner."

Gabriel left the kitchen, and Joy breathed a sigh of relief. She could ignore her attraction to Gabriel when he wasn't around. The trick would be to keep her distance when he was at home. She'd have to simply keep remembering that he was dating.

***

"Strike. You're out," Aretemus Maximillion Aaronson yelled.

"You're blind, Ref. That was a ball, not a strike." Joy stormed over to her brother Max and stood, nose to nose with him. Nose to chin was a better description, but being shorter had never stopped her.

"My call stands," Max said stubbornly.

"Well, we better ask Grace to make an appointment with an optometrist for you, 'cause you're going blind."

"Well, better to be blind than unable to hit a perfectly good pitch," came his retort.

"Perfectly good if you were pitching to that oak tree."

When they heard a muffled sob behind them, both adults stopped their fight. "Honey, what's the matter?" Joy asked Sophie.

Sophie was sitting in the grass, her face in her hands. "You're fighting with Max."

"Honey, remember when I told you I didn't fight fair and that I'd learned that from my brothers?" Joy asked, as she dropped to her knees in front of the child.

Sophie nodded.

"Well, I guess I didn't explain it well enough. Max and I like fighting. It's even more fun when Nick's here, too. We do fight all the time. When we were kids, my mom would come out and yell at us. *You're driving me crazy,* she'd scream. Then, a lot of the time, she'd join right in with us. We were a loud family, but it doesn't mean we don't love each other."

"Really?" Sophie asked, with a small sniffle.

"Honest and truly." Joy crossed her heart and held up a scout sign.

In a hushed voice, Sophie said, "I was little, but I remember Mother and Daddy used to fight all the time, and they don't like each other at all."

Joy was at a loss for how to explain the difference. "Honey, your mother and father fought because they wanted different things and couldn't find any way for both of them to get what they wanted. So they fought and finally decided they would be happier if they both went their own way."

Struggling for a way to explain falling out of love to a six-year-old, Joy continued. "Now, Max and I, we just like to fight. It's our way of saying, *I love you.* He's a boy and never liked to say it to a girl, and I was a little sister who wouldn't be caught dead saying those words to the older brother, so we fight."

"Really?"

"Honest and truly. You remember the other day when we got your daddy by jumping out and yelling boo? Well, we didn't do it because we didn't like him, but because we did. I know it's confusing, but life's often confusing, even when you're big. So, if you don't understand, you ask. I might not know all the answers, but I'll try to figure something out." Joy gave Sophie a hug and pulled her to her feet.

"Okay." Looking shyly at Max who had stayed in the background while Joy talked to her, Sophie said, "And it was a ball, not a strike." It wasn't exactly a shout, but it did Joy good to hear it.

Max looked stricken. "Oh, no, she's warped you already. Has Joy ever told you what I do to little girls who can't tell a ball from a strike?"

Sophie looked a little worried and shook her head.

"I tickle them," Max shouted and gave chase.

Sophie shrieked and raced across the yard. Joy made her

way to the back porch where Grace.

"He's such a big kid," Grace laughed.

Max had done a brilliant stumble, and Sophie was standing a couple yards away, uncertain what to do.

"Tickle him," Joy shouted. "He hates it if you tickle his sides."

"Traitor," Max screamed as Sophie overcame the last of her reticence and attacked.

"She's a beautiful little girl." Grace stood and entered the house, beckoning Joy into the kitchen.

"Yes, she is. I'm afraid I've quite lost my heart to her," Joy said, following her inside and sitting down at the kitchen table.

"And her father?" Grace took the seat opposite Joy.

Joy studied her very innocent-looking sister-in-law. Grace's blonde-haired, blue-eyed features gave her an air of innocence, but the intensity of her gaze made Joy suspect that she knew more about what was going on then she'd admitted. "He's a toad. A total antithesis of one of your storybook heros."

"He is not. Why Blossom has done nothing but swoon over Gabriel since—" She caught herself. "You tricked me!"

"They truly are real?"

Grace nodded. "And Gabriel St. John is not a toad."

"He might as well be, because he's not for me. In case your fairy spies—"

"We resent that term." Myrtle, Fern and Blossom were suddenly sitting in the chairs around the table.

Fern looked stricken. "Grace asked, and we just said he was passable."

"Passable? He's more than passable. He's gorgeous." Joy paused as she realized what she'd said. "I can see I'm not the only tricky one."

Blossom smiled triumphantly. "We knew you liked him."

"Liking him and wanting him are two different things." She didn't add that wanting him was becoming more and more of a possibility. "And, getting him is even harder since you're all ignoring the fact that he has a girlfriend. A girlfriend he's spending the evening with, in case you all forgot."

"They couldn't be out on a date if Helen had a disease. Joy

won't let us give her one," Blossom complained to Grace. "Not even a little one."

"I don't blame her. Do you remember what happened to Susan?"

"You promised you weren't going to mention that anymore." Blossom frowned.

"No. You asked me not to mention it, but I never promised."

"Well, you should have."

"Now, now," Myrtle soothed. "Everything turned out just fine for Susan and Cap *after* she recovered from the mono. And we didn't stop by to discuss our previous adventures. Joy, dear, we just popped in for a quick hello and to let you know we finally have a plan."

"Better ask them what it is," Grace prompted.

Joy was torn with the desire to know, and a fear of what the plan might be. She sighed and asked, "What is it?"

"Oh, now, darling. Don't you worry about it. We have things under control." Fern patted her hand. "And Gabriel did kiss you Thursday night, after all."

"A chaste goodnight kiss on the forehead. He could have given it to Sophie, for Pete's sake. And he's out on a date with Helen, in case you've forgotten."

"Oh, no. We didn't forget. It's part of our plan," Blossom promised.

"What plan?"

"Bye Joy, bye Grace." And the three fairies were gone.

"Do you know what they're up to?" Joy asked her sister-in-law.

"Not a clue."

"Would you tell me if you did?"

Rather than answer the question, Grace said, "So, tell me about this Helen. What's wrong with her?"

"Wrong with her? Why nothing. She's tall, willowy and beautiful. I'm sure she's just what Gabriel's looking for. Actually, she reminds me quite a bit of Trudi, his ex-wife. He must like the type."

"And other than being beautiful, what type is that?"

Joy just shrugged. What she wanted to say was shallow,

arrogant and self-centered, but she didn't. It wouldn't have been fair. Oh, she thought the adjectives safely described Trudi, but she'd spent time with her and had had an opportunity to make that assessment. She had only met Helen once.

She tried to be fair, even when she didn't like it, so she just shrugged. "I don't think our first meeting went very well, so I'm reserving judgement. Suffice it to say, I doubt Helen and I will be best friends."

"Then I guess I don't like her already."

***

"So out with it," Max said as the evening was drawing to a close. They were alone in the kitchen doing dinner dishes. Grace had taken Sophie with her to give Charity her bath. "I want the whole story."

"I told you the whole story." How could she explain to Max why she had stayed when she hardly understood herself. "I couldn't just leave her, Max. She's been uprooted and she's not sure anyone wants her. She became attached to me, and I couldn't walk away from her. She needs me."

Maybe that was the answer. What she hadn't said was that it was a nice feeling to be needed. Max and Nick had been older, so much more sure of their futures. They never really needed a little sister. Her parents functioned more as one person than as two individuals. Though she'd never doubted they loved her, they never really needed her.

Joy needed to be needed.

Drying the dish Max had passed her, Joy probed deeper. Maybe that need was why she started Ripples? The people the foundation helped needed her and the services Ripples could provide. Did that make her selfish? Maybe she wasn't altruistic, but self-serving.

"Joy?" Max asked. She realized the dish in her hands was long dried. She'd have to think about the question later.

"Hmm?"

"I said, what is it you need?"

Joy picked up another plate. "Trust a psychiatrist to ask a question like that. Well, Artemus..." She used his hated first name to needle him. "If you want to analyze me, analyze why

I'm seeing fairies. Or better yet, analyze yourself and figure out why it is you, a man of science, have accepted that three fairies really exist."

He ignored her comment and said, "The only reason I'm letting you go back there—"

"Letting me?" she gasped, outraged.

He scowled at her. "Yes. Letting you. You may be an independent woman, but I'm your big brother. And those fairies are the only reason I'm letting you go back. They don't believe in casual sex."

"Funny, neither do I," Joy mumbled. Her mother and father could be trying, but not even they could surpass Max and Nick in protectiveness.

"They'll want you married first," Max continued, as if she hadn't said a thing.

Joy grabbed another plate. "And since I'm not in Helen's, or even his ex-wife Trudi's league, I don't think you have to worry about us getting married."

"What do you mean not in their league?" Max rinsed a bowl and placed it in the strainer. "We're not exactly paupers."

"That's not what I'm talking about."

With a brotherly tenderness that forced tears to clog her throat, Max lifted her chin. "Joy?"

"Max, I'm too round, too clumsy, too...just too everything that isn't glamorous. It's one of the reasons I'm so good at raising money. Women don't see me as a threat, and men think I'm cute. Maybe just once I'd like to know what it's like to be one of the Helens or Trudis of the world, and have a man drool over me."

"Done," came a trio of voices, though no fairies were visible.

Darn. Joy wasn't used to being eavesdropped on. "Max, did you hear that?"

He shook his head.

"I heard the fairies. They said, 'Done.' You don't think they would...I mean they couldn't...could they?"

"Maybe I should have warned you earlier to be careful what you wish for. You never know who's listening."

Joy could only stare at him in horror. What had she done?

Six

"I liked them," Sophie said, smothering a yawn. "Charity was cute. Grace let me rub powder on her belly after her bath, and she giggled."

Joy resisted the urge to glance at the girl. She kept her eyes glued on the dark country road. "I'm glad you had a good time, sugar."

"Do you think, if I ask Daddy, he'll get me a baby like CheChe?"

Joy choked on absolutely nothing. Wouldn't Gabriel love to be asked to supply Sophie's new sibling? Then thinking of Helen being its mother, she frowned. No, she didn't like the thoughts of Helen acting as Sophie's surrogate mother, much less presenting Gabriel with a child. If she had to put a name to the emotion she felt at those thoughts, it would be jealousy, though goodness knew she had no cause to be jealous.

If she was jealous, then she must care for Gabriel. And though she cared for him—if only for Sophie's sake—it wasn't the type of caring that would produce jealousy. They were developing a friendship, nothing more. So she definitely wasn't jealous.

"I think you better hold off asking your father about that baby."

"Maybe for Christmas," Sophie said.

"Stranger things have happened." Anxious to direct the six-year-old onto a safer subject, she said, "Now, keep your eyes out for your Dad's driveway. It's darker than I expected, and I've only driven this way once before."

"There was that big house on the corner and then Daddy's turn." Sophie yawned again. "I remember from before."

Spotting the house Sophie had spoke of, Joy slowed to almost a crawl and found the driveway easily. The lights of the house winked their greeting to her. As the truck wound down the drive, Joy felt the same warm rush she had felt as a child when she returned to her parent's house after being on a trip. It felt like returning home.

She hadn't really felt at home anywhere in years. Her apartment was just a place to stay between where she had been and where she was going—a place that held her bed and her personal things.

Gabriel and Sophie's house wasn't home, she reminded herself. It was just another stop in her travels. In another week or so, Gabriel would have arranged daycare for Sophie. And Joy would be on her way to her next stop.

Her need to travel, to see new things, suddenly dimmed dramatically. The pleasure she had derived from globetrotting had been losing its glow for a while. Suddenly there wasn't even a spark left.

"What is it you need?" Max had asked. Joy thought she heard the fairies whisper an answer—a name—but she wasn't sure she liked their answer at all.

***

"Okay, Diane. Just remember you can have fun and get the job done." Joy juggled the portable phone on her shoulder and peered out the window. She couldn't see Sophie and was worried about what the girl was getting into.

"Yes, you can. He sounds like a nice man." Joy moved to the dining room window, which offered a view of the west side of the yard. No Sophie.

"Diane, if I didn't think you could do the job, I wouldn't have suggested you go in my place. You just remember that, and have fun while you empty their pocketbooks." She hung up the phone. Where was Sophie?

She went to the back door and shouted, "Sophie?"

Fern winked into the yard. This time, she was mere inches high rather than feet high. The change in height made her look like a storybook fairy rather than a small, eccentric human.

"You'd better hurry. She's in the woods," Fern said, then blinked out. Closer to the trees, she shimmered into view again. "This way. Hurry."

"What's wrong with her, Fern?"

"Nothing...yet. But you still have to hurry."

Joy didn't need any further prompting. From deep in the woods she thought she heard a muffled sound. "Sophie?"

About twenty paces into the trees, Joy realized she should have changed from her sandals into sneakers. Afraid Sophie was in trouble, she didn't even think about going back for them. "Sophie, just stay where you are. I'm coming!"

She was going to kill the fairies. She'd been prepared for them bumbling something. She'd read enough of Grace's books to know bumbling was what the fairies did best. Messing up her life was one thing, but messing with Sophie was something else entirely.

Joy heard loud cries and picked up speed. "Just hang on, honey, I'm coming." The cries stopped abruptly. "Which way?" Joy called.

Myrtle's hazy form appeared about twenty yards ahead of Joy. "This way."

Oh yeah, the fairies were dead meat. And no court in the world would convict her. How could she be tried for killing imaginary beings?

"We're as real as you and Sophie," Blossom's voice whispered in her ear.

"Not for long," Joy muttered just before she stumbled onto Sophie. Literally.

"Umph!" Joy cried as she fell among last years leaves, broken branches and twigs.

Sophie was crouched by a fallen log, and through a disoriented haze, Joy realized she'd tripped over the log itself.

Painfully pulling herself into a sitting position, she eyed the child. "Are you okay?" she asked, brushing the worst of last year's leaves from her hair.

Sophie nodded, much to Joy's relief. "Then why didn't you come when I called?"

"I couldn't leave Jay."

"Jay?"

Sophie pointed towards the log. "I asked him if he wanted to come home, and he did. But he was afraid and ran in there."

"Ah, what is Jay?" Joy asked hesitantly. What kind of wild animals haunted the woods in Western Pennsylvania? Deer? Raccoons? Oh, God, didn't she hear something about them carrying rabies? Snakes?

If the fairies were involved in whatever this was, the species wasn't necessarily limited to Pennsylvania or even the United States. They could ship in just about any animal they wanted.

"Sophie?"

Tears filled the little girl's eyes. "He's a kitty. Oh, Joy, he's so tiny. And no one wants him. He was in a bag down by the creek, and I opened it. He ran out. I wanted to pet him, but he ran away. Joy, he's so tiny. I can't leave him out here all alone with no one to love him."

Sensing they weren't just talking about little kitties who were feeling lonely, Joy did the only thing a sane, rational woman could do. "Are you sure you saw him crawl in here?" Her hand was already poised by the opening of the hole.

Sophie nodded. "I almost had him, but he ran in there. He's fast."

"Okay, here goes." Joy stuck her hand in the hole, expecting to hit kitten fur or the back of the hole quickly, but all she felt was empty space. Images of snakes and bugs and every creepy crawly thing she'd ever seen on public television nature shows flashed through her mind as her arm snaked into the hole past the elbow. "You're sure?"

Sophie nodded again. "It's a big hole. I reached and reached, but couldn't find him."

Knowing there wasn't anything else to do but go for it, Joy lay down on the damp ground and thrust her arm in. It was swallowed up to the shoulder, and she was rewarded by something that felt soft and fuzzy. Praying it wasn't something moldy, or that the kitty Sophie had found—which Joy suspected the fairies had supplied—wasn't a tiger, Joy grasped it.

It wiggled. Joy was pretty sure it wasn't mold. Then it bit. Tiny, sharp, needle-like teeth sank into her skin. A tiger seemed a reasonable guess.

"Ow," she cried, but didn't release her hold. "Come on, Jay. There's a little girl out here who's awfully worried about you."

She pulled, and suddenly a small mass of dirt and fur was hissing in her face, which was still at ground level. Not a tiger, but a tiger-striped kitten.

"Ta dum," she sang and raised herself and the muddy dervish for Sophie to admire. "I think Jay really needs a bath."

"Can I keep him?" The question was asked with hesitancy, as if Sophie expected to be told no.

More than anything, Joy wished she had the right to shout *yes*. But she didn't. She was just a surrogate babysitter. "Well, that will be up to your father."

Sophie's face fell, and Joy added, "But maybe, if we clean him up and show your father what a fine gentleman Jay can be, he'll say yes. If not..." Joy should have hesitated. She should have thought before she spoke, but of their own volition the words tumbled out. "If not, then I guess Jay will have to live with me."

She sent a silent plea to the fairies that Gabriel would see how important it was for him to say yes. Not just because Sophie needed a pet for reassurance, but because Joy didn't need a kitten traveling with her.

"Yes, I'm sure our chances are better if Jay is clean," she said. " So what do you say we go give Jay a bath and teach him how to be a gentleman."

At that moment their future gentleman sank his teeth into a fresh part of Joy's hand. "Ow," she yelped and gently disengaged his jaws. "I think we're going to have to start by showing Jay that gentlemen do not bite ladies, especially not ladies who just saved their life."

"I can carry him," Sophie offered.

Thinking of Jay's carnivorous habits, Joy shook her head.

"How about I carry him until he's been bathed and fed, then you can take over. Okay?"

"Okay."

It didn't take long for Joy to discover a very important fact: *Cats do not like baths.* It didn't matter that Jay was just a kitten. His yowls were pitiful, his claws were accurate, and, to make matters worse, Sophie was right—he was fast. Very, very fast.

"Sophie, grab a couple more towels," Joy shouted.

"Yowl," screamed Jay.

"Don't hurt him," Sophie cried.

Hurt him? Sophie was worried that Joy was going to hurt the tiny hurricane on claws?

"I..." Joy dodged a swatting claw. "Don't..." And put the kitten on the bath mat, pinning him to it with her left hand. "Think..." And tossed a towel over him. He wasn't impressed and hissed beneath it. "Hurting him is my first concern."

The fluffy green towel slithered across the mat. Joy picked it up and started to gently rub the kitten dry. She caught a glance of her reflection in the mirror and sighed. With this little fairy-induced incident—and she was sure they were to blame—she had brought her disaster-itis to a brand new level.

Her hair was littered with half the woods. There were scratches and mud covering every piece of exposed skin. She glanced down at her feet and shuddered. They didn't hurt yet, but the small twinges coming from their direction told her that they were going to hurt in the morning. Wearing sandals for an afternoon jaunt in the woods wasn't the wisest thing for a woman to do.

"Sophie, I think we better finish with Jay and try to get things cleaned up before your father..." She broke off when there was a knock at the bathroom door.

Maybe it was the fairies? Oh, goodness, she hoped it was the fairies.

"Sophie? Joy?"

"Uh oh," two voices groaned in unison as Jay yowled.

So much for fairy godmothers looking out for her. Innocently, Joy called, "Yes?"

"What are you two doing? There's mud all over downstairs."

"I..." She couldn't think of a single worthwhile explanation. Realizing it was time to face the music, she rose. Clutching the towel-covered cause of her embarrassment close to her chest, she opened the door. "I guess you want an explanation?"

She was hoping he'd say no, but didn't hold out much hope, and he didn't disappoint her.

"Yes."

"It's all my fault. You see—"

Sophie pushed past Joy and ran to her father. Gabriel knelt and Sophie wrapped her arms around his neck. "Daddy, I found Jay, but I couldn't get him out and Joy did and she said she couldn't say yes, but you could. But if you don't she'll take him. But don't say no 'cause I want him. He loves me and needs me and when Joy goes..." Sophie's voice broke slightly. "When Joy goes back to her work, she'll still love me, 'cause we're kindred spirits, but Jay would still be here to love me 'cause he'll be mine."

"Well, that clears up a lot." Gabriel pulled Sophie close for another hug. "Why don't you run to your room and change your clothes? Joy and I will try to sort this out."

Sophie broke away from his embrace. "Just don't say no, okay?" she whispered and then hurried down the hall to her room.

"I'm lost," Gabriel murmured as he rose, his gaze holding Joy's. Her heart did a little flip-flop. The kitten echoed it, flip-flopping in the towel at her chest. "Maybe you could explain all this?"

"Jay's a kitten. He got stuck in a hole in a log and I got him out." Gently she lifted an edge of the towel and the cleaned kitten, who had turned velvety orange with stripes, peeked out. "Sophie's in love and wants to keep him. I told her if you said no he could live with me, but since I travel so much I'd rather not have to honor that particular promise."

Gabriel didn't say a word, but simply took the wet mass of orange fur, towel and all, from her. "Well, you're a mighty fine looking fella." He scratched under the kitten's chin. "And my

Sophie's fallen for you, eh?" He looked Joy up and down. "Sophie might have fallen for him, but it looks like you took a fall or two yourself."

"It'll wash off." It was as if Gabriel was suddenly looking into the center of her being and liked what he saw. His hand continued stroking the kitten as his eyes seemed to stroke her.

"Speaking of washing...if you wouldn't mind kitten-sitting, I'd very much like to see if I could do some myself."

Gabriel's fingers left the kitten, and he reached out and lightly ran a finger down her jaw-line.

His touch sent unexpected sparks flying through Joy's system. "gabriel?" she whispered, unsure what she was asking, but sure that she wanted him to answer.

He dropped his hand. "I can put something on these scratches so they don't get infected."

"Oh." Joy had wanted something from Gabriel—something she couldn't quite name. But concern over her scratches definitely wasn't it. "Thanks, but I'm sure I can handle it."

He simply nodded and, taking the kitten, left the bathroom.

Joy began to shut the door, but Gabriel's foot in the doorjamb stopped her. "We need to talk tonight."

"Sure. After Sophie's in bed." She whirled into the bathroom and shut the door. Her heart was hammering, and her knees were shaking. "What have the three of you done?" she whispered.

Three fairies, in bathing suits and swim caps, lined the edge of the tub. "Just sent down a little cat."

"Mountain lion," Joy corrected. "And I already guessed that. But, what have you done to Gabriel?"

"*Done?*" A slow smile spread over Blossom's face.

"Done. He's never looked at me like that before."

"Like what?" asked Fern.

"Like he could read my thoughts as easily as you three do."

"We don't have the power to let him do something like that." Myrtle raised her hand. "Scouts honor."

"Were you three ever scouts?"

"Fairy scouts. It's where all godmothers start. First scouts, than fairy sisters, and finally, fairy godmothers. Though godmothers tend to work solo." Blossom looked puzzled. "For some reason the council decided to leave the three of us together."

"Just go away, girls. I'm not Gabriel's type, and nothing you can do is going to change that."

***

Joy.

The name seemed to be embedded in Gabriel's mind, along with the mental image of her clutching the kitten, her big blue eyes begging him not to disappoint Sophie. And maybe they were asking him not to disappoint her, either.

Like a magnet, he was drawn to her. The attraction seemed to grow by leaps and bounds every day—every minute—he spent with her. He spied her curled on the couch, one throw pillow under her head, another in her arms, her body curled around it. Her hair was feathered over the pillow, spilling over the edge of the couch. She had kept it pulled back since he met her. Gabriel was surprised by its length. The warm brown color, with its honey streaks, suited her. Suited him.

Gabriel found himself noticing a lot of things about Joy that he doubted he would have noticed about anyone else. Her physical features were appealing enough, but it was what couldn't be seen that Gabriel noticed most of all. Joy seemed to have more room in her heart than anyone he'd ever met. Again, he remembered how she had looked, covered in dirt and scratches, with the kitten clutched to her chest. He couldn't remember any woman ever looking so lovely.

"Hi," he said.

"Hi. You get Sophie to sleep?" Joy asked, smothering a yawn.

"Well, after listening to half an hour's complaints that I don't read the book right, I kissed her head and told her to go to sleep."

Joy chuckled. "Did she go to sleep?"

Gabriel shrugged and plopped into the recliner. "No idea. I just shut the door and made my escape. And are you going to tell me how to read a story the right way?"

"Voices." Joy pulled herself up into a sitting position. There were lines from the pillow on her cheek, and she brushed a stray hair behind her ear.

Gabriel swallowed hard. His palms were suddenly damp with sweat. He felt nervous in a way he hadn't felt since his teens. "Uh, voices?"

"Yeah, you have to do the voices." Deepening her voice, Joy cackled, "*And you will fall into a deep sleep and never awaken.*" She let another round of high cackles rain through the room.

Gabriel gave a mock shudder. "Oh, voices."

"That's the trick. I was younger than my brothers, Max and Nick, and they read to me whenever Mom was out. Max was my favorite. He did the voices."

"I'll remember that." He reached for the remote and clicked off the television. "I need to talk to you."

"That's what you said. Sophie's in bed and the living room is ours, so you have the floor."

"It's about someone to babysit for Sophie. I started making inquiries. There are a couple ladies that babysit for kids in their homes. Both of them say they can take Sophie full-time until school starts, and this fall she can go to their homes after school. I hoped you might go with me tomorrow afternoon and check them out." Gabriel didn't like the idea of leaving Sophie with strangers, but there wasn't much he could do about it.

A thought suddenly hit him. Joy was a stranger, and he'd never minded leaving Sophie with her. Why was that?

Maybe it had something to do with the fact that Joy was so easy to be with. She inspired trust. She seemed sweet, easygoing and unaffected, and...well, she was comfortable.

"Sure. Are we taking Sophie with us?"

There was something in her face. It almost looked like pain, but it disappeared as quickly as it had come, and her ever-present smile returned.

"I asked Helen if she'd mind sitting with Sophie while we were gone."

"Oh. That should be...interesting. Are you sure?"

Gabriel smiled. Helen was the most efficient assistant he'd ever had. She handled areas of his life no other personal assistant would dream of taking on, and yet she managed them without complaint or mistakes. Certainly a couple hours with a six-year-old would be no problem. "I'm sure Helen will do fine."

Joy just shrugged as she yawned and gave a little stretch. "I'm going to turn in early tonight. Sophie's running me ragged." She got off the couch and walked gingerly towards the stairs.

"What's the matter with your legs?" Gabriel asked.

"Feet. When I ran through the woods today, I had on sandals and managed to bang them up a little."

By the way she was walking, it looked like she had banged them up a lot. "Sit down on the couch and let me have a look."

"They're fine, really. Just a little bit sore." She shuffled towards the stairs.

"Sit down, Joy." She didn't listen. He took back every thought he'd just had about Joy being easy-going. She was stubborn as a mule. Did she think she had to do everything by herself?

"Gabriel, really I'm okay."

"Sit."

She turned around, shuffled back to the couch and sat. Gabriel sat down next to her and pulled her foot onto his lap. He peeled off her sock and held his breath. "What the hell were you thinking?" He probed the small cuts that were sprinkled over the sides and top of her foot.

"I was thinking that I couldn't see Sophie. I was thinking she could be hurt, and I just ran. I wasn't going back for sneakers." She winced as he lightly traced the deepest cut.

Gabriel could hardly argue with her rationale, but he still hated seeing the cuts on her foot. He pulled off the other sock, and this time he let out a long whistle. "Did you put something on this?"

"Peroxide." She grunted as his fingers ran over her insole. Her perpetual smile was replaced by a grimace.

"It should have been bandaged." He probed the two-inch cut running along the outside of her foot.

"I couldn't find anything long enough to cover the whole thing."

Gently he moved her feet from his lap and stomped up the stairs. That cut must have hurt, but she hadn't said anything.

She'd showered, changed, and rigged up an impromptu litter box for the kitten. Then she had helped serve the dinner she had going in the crock pot—it had been years since he'd had chicken and dumplings. She'd still managed to help with dinner dishes, take a call from someone at Ripples and get Sophie off to bed.

The whole time it must have hurt to be on her feet. Swearing about stubborn females who didn't know how to ask for help, Gabriel pulled some gauze from the back of the cupboard and went scrounging for the tape. At the last minute, he grabbed the antibiotic cream.

He went down the stairs and sat on the couch. "Give me your foot."

"Oh, if you have the gauze that's big enough, I can put it on myself."

"Give me your foot," he repeated, then threw in a "Please?" when it looked like she was still going to argue.

Frowning, she practically threw her foot onto his lap. "There."

"Thank you." He dabbed the cream on the cut.

"Ow," she muttered. "That hurts."

He dabbed more gently. It had been a long time since he'd doctored someone. "I'm sorry it hurt. Do you want a kiss to make it feel better? That always works for Sophie."

Her face paled, and Gabriel wondered what was going through her head. He was never quite sure. The only thing he was sure of was that she fascinated him, and the fascination was growing by leaps and bounds every day.

"I don't think any kissing is necessary. Actually, it's already feeling better. Thanks."

"Just part of the service. But, I still think a kiss might help."

"Ah, but you don't want to kiss my foot." Joy scooted back on the couch.

"Maybe we'd both be a little more comfortable if I kissed you somewhere else."

He swung her bandaged foot to the ground and reached for her, pulling her closer to him. "Let's see if this makes it feel better."

"Gabriel..." Whether it was a protest or an invitation, he didn't know, but the minute his lips met hers, he didn't care. Tenderness was quickly overshadowed by need as his lips urgently explored hers.

"Daddy, I need a drink."

Reluctantly, Gabriel tore himself away from Joy. What sort of spell had this woman cast over him? "Wait here," he said. "We obviously have more to talk about."

He glanced over his shoulder as he climbed the stairs. Joy was sitting on the couch looking lost. Though he felt as confused as she looked, Gabriel knew that he wouldn't undo that kiss, even if he could.

As a matter of fact, he'd like to repeat it as soon as he'd given Sophie her drink.

Hurriedly, he gave her the water and retucked her in her bed. But when he returned to the living room, Joy was gone.

He knew instinctively that she was running from whatever was happening between them.

Gabriel smiled. She could run, but he wasn't giving up. Eventually he'd catch her and see just what these feelings blazing between them meant.

Sophie might have brought them together, but Sophie didn't play into what he was feeling for Joy now. He couldn't quite define those feelings. But Gabriel knew that Joy Aaronson was the most fascinating woman he'd ever met.

Seven

"No," Joy said.

"I thought Mrs. Francis seemed nice enough," Gabriel insisted as he navigated the car along the winding dirt road.

"She has six kids of her own—"

"Which means she has experience."

"—And, she watches two others."

"To help make the financial ends meet without leaving her children with someone else while she works outside the house."

"What kind of personal attention would Sophie get with eight other children to compete with? What if she wanted someone to read to her? Can you really see Mrs. Francis having time to read, much less to do—"

"The voices," Gabriel finished for her and sighed. "You're right."

"Sophie doesn't need Mrs. Francis or anyone else," Blossom said.

Joy stifled a groan and tried to sneak a peek into the back seat. The fairies cheerily waved at her.

"Hi, Joy," Fern said. "We won't embarrass you in front of Gabriel, so you can stop worrying. Just don't talk back to us, and he'll never know we're here."

"And, Blossom's right," Myrtle said. "Sophie doesn't need Mrs. Francis. She needs you."

"It's not my decision," Joy said to Gabriel for the fairies' benefit. "And you did have a point. Mrs. Francis seemed nice enough and certainly does know a thing or two about kids." She shot a glare at the back seat.

"You're wrong," three fairies said in unison.

"Joy, I said, you were right," Gabriel said at the same time.

"Maybe not. I mean, maybe Sophie would enjoy being in the middle of all those kids. She might not miss the stories because she'd be so busy with everything that's bound to go on when there are eight children together, nine counting her." She paused. "I..." her voice trailed off, as she stared at his lips. They'd ignored the kiss. Neither had mentioned it. But all day his lips had distracted her.

"See, Joy wants another kiss," Fern said excitedly.

"Just kiss him," Blossom encouraged.

She could ignore the kiss if he could. Too bad she couldn't ignore the fairies.

"I should hope not," Myrtle said.

Their ability to read her mind was annoying.

"Not as annoying as goddaughters who ignore their feelings," Myrtle said. "You know you want to kiss him again.

Joy was determined to ignore any thoughts of kissing. She might ignore the kiss, but she knew she couldn't forget it. As much as she knew things between them could never work out, Joy planned to remember that kiss for the rest of her life—when it was safe. And it wouldn't be safe until the fairies were gone.

"But we're not going anywhere," Myrtle assured her.

"At least not until you and Gabriel are settled," Fern added.

Between fantasizing about Gabriel's lips and worrying about the fairies, Joy was becoming a basket case.

Gabriel pulled to the side of the road and turned towards her, his frustration written on his face. "Joy, I agreed with you. I think Sophie should be with someone who can focus more attention on her. She's been through so much and—"

"She needs to feel secure and needs someone who can understand that." Joy wanted someone like that in her life as well. Instead she had three fairies.

"Kiss him, kiss him," the fairies quietly chanted, like some insane cheerleading squad.

"We both agree, so why are we arguing?" Gabriel asked.

Agree to kissing? No, they were talking about babysitters, not kissing. "I'm not arguing, I'm just discussing. You're the one who's getting all upset."

And Joy was the one who was having trouble concentrating on anything but Gabriel St. John's lips. She'd like to have another taste, just to be sure the kiss was everything her memory was playing it up to be. But she knew she couldn't afford to kiss him again. He had Helen, and Joy was leaving as soon as they found a sitter.

"Helen doesn't look very kissable," Blossom said.

"Sort of cold and aloof," Fern added.

Gabriel said, "It's just that you didn't like Mrs. Francis because she had too many kids. You didn't like Terry because she didn't have any."

"And she was only eighteen." She didn't add that Terry was stacked and had been giving Gabriel looks that spoke of more than a desire to babysit.

"Ha, jealousy. That's a good sign," Myrtle said. "First you were jealous of Helen, now you're jealous of Terry. Yes, that's a very good sign."

"Eighteen is old enough to watch a child for a couple weeks," Gabriel argued, not for the first time.

She wasn't jealous, just like she wasn't going to kiss Gabriel St. John.

"Oh, yes you are. Sooner than you think," Myrtle said merrily.

Joy ignored the desire to throttle a trio of fairies, which was almost as difficult as ignoring her desire to kiss Gabriel. "Who watches Sophie is your decision. You're her father. I'm just along for the ride."

"I want your opinion. You seem to understand Sophie much better than I do. It's just that yesterday you didn't like Starling or Mrs. Matson, either."

"One was named after a bird and looked like a young vampire."

"She did not," he said, more humor than annoyance in his voice.

"She was dressed all in black and...well, hell Gabriel, she was scary. And Mrs. Matson was at least eighty—"

"—seventy-one, and the grandmother of thirteen."

"—and with her walker, she couldn't have chased Sophie if her life depended on it. As a matter of fact, if she'd tried to chase Sophie, it might have been her life." Joy had a feeling she would never find anyone who would be good enough for Sophie, but it wouldn't do to tell Gabriel that. She'd have to try harder to be impartial, but being impartial was next to impossible where Gabriel and Sophie were concerned.

"Like we said, Sophie needs you," Myrtle said. "And so does Gabriel."

"And if you'd stop fighting your destiny, you'd see that maybe you need both of them as well," Blossom said.

"Fine, so what do I do now?" Gabriel asked.

"You keep looking." She'd do better, she swore to herself, ignoring the fairies. Gabriel was right. It was only a few more weeks until school started, and she was being way too picky.

"Because you care," Fern said.

"And in the meantime?" Gabriel asked.

"You kiss," the three fairies said in unison.

"We make it work." *With no kissing*, Joy added silently.

"I'll juggle Ripples, don't worry."

"Joy, I can't ask you to continue putting your life on hold. Helen can always help me out." He turned back to the wheel and eased the car back onto the road.

"I've never asked, but just what does Helen do?" Joy had avoided mentioning Helen's name. She felt guilty for kissing a man who was involved with someone else.

"She works for me. I thought you knew that."

"Oh." How convenient. His girlfriend worked for him. Just what kind of work did they do all day long? Business or *business*? Joy's imagination was suddenly filled with images of Helen and Gabriel taking care of *business* in the office. Not that it was any of her concern what they did. They were two consenting adults.

"You could always consent to a few more of Gabriel's kisses, and then there would be no worry about Helen," Fern said.

"Anyway, I'll ask Helen. It would be great for her to spend more time with Sophie. Look how well they managed yesterday. I'm sure it went just as well today," he said with a smile.

"Yeah, sure it did," Blossom giggled.

Joy paled. What were the fairies up to now?

"Nothing, Joy. We didn't do anything," Myrtle assured her. "But since you're not kissing Gabriel, we'd better go."

Joy wished she could scream for them to stay right where they were. She had a bad feeling about Helen and Sophie. Fifteen minutes later, they pulled into the driveway of Gabriel's house. The bad feeling intensified when she saw smoke streaming out the living room windows.

"What the hell?" Gabriel swore as he jumped from the car and ran towards the house.

Joy reached over and turned off the ignition, which he'd failed to do, and hurried out her own door. A blaring noise came from the house.

"Sophie?" she called.

The smell of smoke was almost overwhelming as she entered the door, but underneath it, there was a smell of something else, something...

"Daddy! Joy!" Sophie screamed, rushing towards them. Joy released the breath she hadn't realized she'd been holding, then deeply regretted that she had.

The smoke was definitely coming from the kitchen. "Gabriel, help!" came a scream.

"Dinner's served," Joy said, smiling at Gabriel.

Helen appeared from the midst of the smoke. "I burned dinner and can't get rid of the smoke, and that damned alarm won't shut up."

"Joy, could you—"

"Take Sophie outside while you help Helen clean up? Sure."

"That's not what I was going to ask," he grumbled.

"I know, but that's what I'm going to do." She scooped up the little girl and headed toward the door and the breathable air outside.

"Hey, that's not fair," Gabriel said, even as he started towards the vile-smelling kitchen. Gabriel's obvious annoyance at having to clean up Helen's mess did nothing to lift her spirits. As a matter of fact, she had the urge to go help him, but she ignored it. Just as she'd ignored all the feelings that were continually fluttering around, turning her inside to jelly. Gabriel had Helen. Joy had Ripples. That was what she told herself for what must have been the millionth time.

Her head seemed to be listening.

It was her heart that was ignoring it.

Gabriel watched Joy and Sophie make their escape, his gaze resting on the slight sway of Joy's hips as she moved. He sighed and looked around the smoky kitchen. "Well, let's see if we can shut off that alarm and clean up the kitchen."

Ten minutes later, with all the windows opened, things were much better.

"Gabriel, I'm so sorry," Helen said for the hundredth time. "I thought you'd be surprised if I had dinner waiting for you."

"I promise you, I was surprised."

"I guess I'm just not domestic. The man at the store promised me that anyone could broil steaks."

Gabriel felt a stab of sympathy for his assistant. Helen was so very capable at just about anything he asked of her. "It's nice to find there's something you can't do."

"Don't tell anyone, okay?" She laughed.

"Sure." They worked in silence, cleaning the charred remains of the steaks out of the stove. Gabriel's mind turned from burned steaks to the small woman he'd spent the day with. All day long he'd been plagued with thoughts of kissing her again. Kissing her and more—much more. But Joy had kept her distance, and though she seemed to be her normal, friendly self, Gabriel could sense that something had changed.

Gone was the ease they'd experienced. There was an ever-present tension between them, and he had no idea how to get back to where they'd been those first few days. Actually, Gabriel wasn't sure he wanted to go back to their easy friendliness. Kissing Joy might just be worth the tension.

He'd fantasized about her lips all day. More than that, he'd fantasized about tasting more than just her lips. He wanted to learn every curve of her body, every inch of her. He wanted...damn it, he wanted her. And from all appearances she didn't want him. And yet, when she'd kissed him, he hadn't sensed the wall she seemed to be trying to put up. He'd sensed passion.

The image of Joy lying beneath him, her bright blue eyes reflecting the passion he wanted her to feel, flashed across his mind.

"Gabriel?"

He started and realized Helen was talking to him. "Pardon?"

"I asked if everything is all right? You're awfully quiet."

No, damn it, everything wasn't all right. He couldn't figure Joy Aaronson out. Worse, he couldn't figure himself out. He sighed. "Yeah, everything's fine. Just fine." At least it would be as soon as he could kiss Joy again.

"Can you steady the ladder while I put the battery back in the smoke alarm? I think the smoke's cleared enough to turn it back on."

"Helen, I can do that."

"Nonsense. This ladder wasn't meant for someone as big as you. Just hold it."

Gabriel grabbed at the small step stool which wobbled under Helen's slight weight.

"Gabriel!" she shrieked as the ladder began to topple.

Gabriel caught his free-falling assistant. "I told you I should have done that," he scolded, as he lowered her feet to the floor.

Helen laughed. "I knew you'd catch me if I fell."

"How's everything going?"

Gabriel turned at the sound of Joy's voice. He realized his arm was still around Helen and dropped it guiltily. "Fine. Everything's just fine."

Joy studied them both a moment and simply nodded. "Sophie and I decided to call for pizza."

"Great. Whatever you want."

She nodded and walked silently from the room.

"I don't think your babysitter likes me," Helen said.

"Of course she likes you."

"Men," Helen grumbled.

He turned and studied Helen. "What do you mean by that crack?"

"I mean, Boss, that Joy doesn't like me at all, and it's nothing personal, believe me."

"What is it then?"

"You're a big boy, you figure it out."

And with that, his mouthy assistant left the room.

Women. Who could figure them out? Certainly not Gabriel St. John. He didn't have a clue. But he knew one thing—he desperately wanted to kiss Joy Aaronson again.

Joy had told Sophie that she learned to fight dirty from her brothers. Well, Gabriel was going to take a lesson from Joy and those brothers. He wanted another kiss, and he wasn't above fighting dirty to get one.

***

Men? Who could figure them out. Gabriel had been behaving strangely since yesterday. Joy glanced his way, and quickly turned her attention back to the woman across the table. It was easier to think about interviewing a babysitter for Sophie than to try to figure out what was going on in Gabriel's head.

"If and when discipline is necessary, how you do believe it should be handled?" Joy frowned as Eloise McDaniels considered the question thoughtfully. It might not have been so irritating if the woman hadn't deliberated over each question as if her life depended on the answer.

"Miss Aaronson, I'm sure I'll have little difficulty with Sophie, but when and if some major form of discipline is required, I believe time outs are the most effective. Occasionally, if the situation warrants it, denying some small pleasure also works well."

"I...Well..." Joy couldn't think of any other questions to ask. "Gabriel?" she deferred.

"Thank you, Ms. McDaniels. We'll be making our decision soon and will let you know either way."

It wasn't until they were out on the sidewalk that Gabriel asked, "Well, what's wrong with this one?"

"Now, why would you assume I'd find fault with her? From all appearances, she's just what you need. Not only can she take care of Sophie until school starts, but she's available to watch her after school. She's fifty—she taught first-grade for almost thirty years. She's married, but all her children have left home. She doesn't believe in physical discipline, she knows how to make chocolate chip cookies and...well, hell, Gabriel, she'll even do the voices when she reads." It pained her, but Joy admitted, "She's perfect, and she'll start on Monday."

If she didn't know the fairies didn't want her to leave and spoil their plans for a-happily-ever-after with Gabriel, she'd say Ms. McDaniels was perfect enough to be fairy-sent.

"You're not going to comment on her frilly outfit or that annoying way she deliberated over every question?" he asked.

Joy shook her head as she climbed into the car.

Gabriel started the engine. "You're not going to wonder if her love of cookie-making will be bad for Sophie's nutritional health?" he continued.

"Gabriel, I'm sure a few cookies aren't going to hurt Sophie."

"Nothing?" He almost sounded disappointed as he drove toward home.

"I told you, Ms. McDaniels seems perfect for you, and I'm sure that Sophie will learn to love her." And as much as Joy hoped it was so, part of her hoped Sophie didn't learn to love Eloise McDaniels as much as she loved Joy. It was a small petty, part—one that Joy had never realized existed—and one that she tapped back down as quickly as possible.

Summoning up every ounce of her courage, she said, "Unless you have a problem with something I didn't notice, I suggest you snatch her up. I can call work and arrange to be back in the office on Monday."

Gabriel turned and just looked at her. "I guess you're right. I'll call her tonight and give her the news." Turning his gaze back to the road he said, "I don't know how I'll ever thank you for all—"

"Gabriel, that's not necessary. Truth be known, this has been the first decent vacation I've had in years. I've loved..." Joy felt something suspiciously like tears gathering in her eyes, and she blinked to hold them back. "I've loved every minute of it. It's I who should be thanking you."

"Fine, we're a mutual admiration club here." His eyes left the road and met hers. "And I do admire you."

"I..." Joy knew what she felt for Gabriel was more than

admiration, but Helen stood between them. The image of Gabriel and Helen in the kitchen was burned into her mind—his arm casually draped around her. She was the woman he should be with. The kiss he'd shared with Joy was just an aberration.

Joy could never be what Gabriel obviously wanted in a woman—someone glamorous and worldly like Helen and Trudi. Joy was just too normal. Gabriel was as brilliant and beautiful as Joy's brothers, and she knew she could never measure up. That's why she'd stopped trying to years ago. She might not be extraordinary, but she'd learned to be comfortable being normal.

"I admire you, too," she managed. "Now, let's go tell Sophie about Ms. McDaniels, and then let's go celebrate."

"What do you suggest?"

"Dinner—on you. Sophie and I get to pick the place."

Chuckling, Gabriel agreed, then suddenly sobered as he said, "Things aren't going to be the same when you're gone."

Joy's heart lurched. She very much feared things would never be the same again for her. "You'll forget all about me in a week or two."

A part of her prayed it wasn't true, even as another part whispered in her brain, *He's got Helen.* She was here because of Sophie. Gabriel had never given her any reason to believe that had changed. So he'd kissed her. Kisses were easily given. Unfortunately, they weren't so easily received, at least not for Joy.

"In just a week or two, you and Sophie will be settled into your new routine. And I'll be a pleasant memory," she whispered. And for the rest of her life, Joy was afraid Gabriel and Sophie would be an unattainable dream.

***

"I don't think I can move," Gabriel groused from his position on the couch. "There are too many steps between here and my room."

Joy shook her head sadly. "You are old, Gabriel. Only a very old man would be so tired after dinner and bowling."

They'd eaten at AMazing Meals, an indoor playground and restaurant. At Sophie's prodding, they spent more time playing than eating.

He scowled at her. "I don't see you bounding up those steps."

"I'm thinking about it. Here I go." She didn't move from the easy chair. "Okay, I'll go in a minute."

"Where does Sophie find the energy?" Gabriel asked.

"I don't know, but do you think if we asked real nice, she'd share it with us?" Joy ached from the top of her head, where she'd banged herself on the slide, to the tip of her toes. Her body was never meant to be twisted and toyed with like AMazing Meals and Sophie St. John had done.

"You know, I'm going to miss you. Both Sophie and I will," he quickly added. "You gave me the greatest gift I've ever received when you brought me back my daughter."

Joy just shrugged off his thanks. It made her uncomfortable. "I didn't do it, Gabriel. Trudi was going to send her back one way or another. I just happened to be in the right place at the right time."

"It was more than that and you know it, but I'm not going to argue. I just wanted to thank you."

"Well, you have, and now it's my turn. Thanks for sharing Sophie with me and for giving me this time with her. She's precious, and I appreciate being allowed a place in her life."

"Like I could keep you out of her life. You're already firmly in her heart."

"Well," she said, rising creakily to her feet. "Thank you anyway. This time with the two of you has been special, and I can't thank you enough for it." She shuffled forward a step. "But right now, if I'm hoping to spend one last day running around with Sophie, I'm off to bed."

"Joy," Gabriel called.

"Yes?" She turned and smiled.

Gabriel looked as if he had something to say and then thought better of it. He simply said, "Good night."

"Good night, Gabriel." That said, Joy hobbled towards her room, her physical pain not even beginning to match the pain that was burning in her heart.

Gabriel watched her go. He'd wanted to wrap Joy in his arms and kiss her senseless. Kiss her until she forgot all about leaving them. Kiss her until she promised to never go. He was right when he'd said he'd miss her. There would be a hole left in his and Sophie's lives. A hole only Joy could fill.

How could they let her leave?

How could he ask her to stay?

And if he asked, would she consider staying? She had a career and a life waiting for her in Chicago. What could he offer her that would entice her to give that up? He'd have to think fast, and fight dirty.

An idea began to form. And for the first time since they'd interviewed Eloise and decided she'd be a suitable babysitter, Gabriel's heart felt light. It looked like there was a chance they wouldn't be needing Eloise at all.

A chance.

That's all Gabriel was asking for.

***

"You're leaving, aren't you?" the little girl whispered Saturday morning.

Joy dropped to her knees and met those sweet eyes dead on. "Yes. Tomorrow. It's time for me to go. Remember, Daddy and I said we found someone to stay with you while he works? Well, that will only be for a few weeks, and then you'll be starting school."

"I'll miss you!" Sophie cried and threw her arms around Joy's neck.

"You'll be so busy when you start school you won't have time to even realize I'm gone." Joy tried to hold back the tears pressing against her eyes.

"I'll miss you with all my heart, just like I missed Daddy when Mother took me away." Sophie gave a little sob against the crook of Joy's neck.

"But I'll call and I'll visit. We'll go back to Max's, and you can play with CheChe and—"

"It won't be the same."

"No. Nothing stays the same. And things don't always go the way we'd like them to, but kindred spirits are never very far apart."

She hugged the little girl tight, continuing to hold back her tears. Finally she moved Sophie back and looked into those beautiful brown eyes that reminded her so much of Gabriel's. "Now, it's time for us to do something special for our last day together. Then we'll come home, and you can help me pack."

Sophie sniffled back her tears. The sound tore at Joy's heart. It was for the best, she'd told herself over and over.

Sophie had Gabriel.

Gabriel had Helen.

Joy had Ripples.

"Come on," Joy said, forcing joviality into her voice. "I have a plan."

Sophie gave another sniffle and eyed Joy suspiciously. "What?"

"We're going on a picnic."

"A picnic?" Sophie said, showing a bit of interest.

"Yeah. I'm going to make my world-famous peanut butter and secret ingredient sandwiches. Then we're going on an adventure."

"Where?"

"It's a secret. We'll make our lunch, and we'll leave a note for your sleepy-head daddy and go." It was probably cowardly to use Sophie as a barrier between herself and Gabriel, but Joy just couldn't face the thought of seeing him. She needed distance. Thoughts of kissing, and even more, had plagued her for days. She had to come to grips with these unrealized, unattainable dreams.

No matter what the fairies said, Gabriel wasn't interested in her that way.

"Why do we have to leave a note?" Sophie asked.

"So he won't worry when he wakes up. You should never scare the people you love like that. You leave a note and let them know where you went and when you'll be home."

"Okay."

They were both in the process of assembling a lunch when Gabriel came down the stairs. "You two should have woke me sooner than this."

"Sorry, we were busy. Coffee's still fresh, though," Joy said over her shoulder. "You can help yourself and relax with the paper. Sophie and I are off to have an adventure."

"An adventure?" he asked groggily.

"We're going on a picnic in the woods, Daddy."

"Just the two of you?" he asked. "Aren't you afraid of bears?"

"Bears?" Sophie whispered.

"There are no bears in the woods," Joy assured her and glared at Gabriel.

"Oh, yes there are. They're big, and they are only afraid of one thing."

"What?" Sophie asked, looking nervously at the two of them, obviously unsure whom to believe.

"Gabriel, you're scaring her," Joy scolded.

Gabriel ignored Joy and concentrated on Sophie. "Daddies. That's what bears are afraid of. If you take a daddy with you, they'll never come near you."

"Really?" Sophie asked.

Gabriel ran his fingers in a cross across his chest. "Honest and truly."

"Men," Joy groused. "If you wanted to come along, you could have asked. You didn't have to scare a six-year-old half to death."

He gave her a funny look. "You might have told me no if you didn't think you needed me."

Joy ignored him and turned to Sophie. "What do you think? Should we take your daddy along as a bear protector?" She glared at Gabriel. "He'd have to pull his weight. I mean, we made the lunch, so he'd have to think of something to offer."

"I could take you to the best picnic area in the whole woods," he volunteered.

"The best?" Sophie asked.

"The very, very best," he said, giving her braids a swat.

"I guess we could take you, if it's okay with Joy," Sophie allowed.

"Well?" he asked Joy.

Part of Joy wanted to shout, *No*, but she couldn't. She needed as much distance as she could get between the two of them, but Sophie needed him there more. It was her last day, so what could happen?

"Don't you have plans with Helen today?" she asked, giving her peace-filled day one more chance.

He shook his head and Joy, recognizing defeat, nodded. "If you really want to come, then I guess we could use some protection from all those bears." She tried to force a smile, but suspected it wasn't very convincing.

Gabriel had them organized and out the door within minutes, and about ten minutes later he shouted, "Ta da." The three of them stood in front of a small creek. "I thought it might be fun to go wading."

"You're right, Daddy, this is the best place." Sophie sat on the ground and whipped off her shoes and socks. "Come on."

Joy set their lunch down and peeled off her sneakers and socks as well. "Have you ever gone skating in a creek?"

"Skating?" Sophie asked.

"Look at that flat rock there. Can you see the green slime on it?" Joy pointed to a long grey piece of slate.

"Ew, slime is slimy," Sophie said, her pert little nose wrinkling.

The creek was shallow and well shaded by the trees that lined its banks. The flat granite rock that the water flowed over was covered with green algae.

"Yeah, and it's slippery. You can slide across it, just like it was ice." Joy was already standing ankle deep in the water.

"Really?" Sophie didn't look convinced that ice skating on slime was a good thing.

"Really. My brothers and I used to do it all the time when we were little." Joy turned to Gabriel, beckoning him to join her. "Are you coming in?"

"I'm not sure I want to go slime skating. I was thinking about doing some plain old, traditional wading."

"He's an old fogey," Joy stage whispered to Sophie.

"What's a fogey?" Sophie asked.

"That's what we call someone who won't try something new." Joy grinned at Gabriel, throwing down the gauntlet.

"Won't try anything new?" That he had accepted the challenge was evident as he leaned down and peeled off his shoes and socks. "Oh, I accept. And I'll show you who is the king of slime skating."

"Yeah, big words from an old fogey." Joy took Sophie's hand, pulling her towards the large, flat rock. "We'll show him."

She and Sophie tripped and giggled as they made their way across the slippery surface.

"Hey, hurry up Daddy. Joy was right, this is fun."

Gabriel didn't look to sure. "It feels gross," he said as he stepped into the water.

"Baby," Joy taunted.

"That's it. You're in for it now." He made a dash—a very unwise thing to do when walking on slime. A very, very unwise thing. That much was apparent as Gabriel began his downward descent.

Joy rushed toward him, though she wasn't sure what she expected to accomplish. What she did accomplish was getting pulled down with him—under him actually—as he hit the floor of the creek. "Gabriel!" she screamed.

Thankfully, the water was shallow, and even pinned beneath him Joy was in no danger of being submerged.

Gabriel didn't say a thing. Actually, he couldn't say a thing because he was laughing so hard. The laughter slowly died and was replaced by an intensity that momentarily stole Joy's breath away. Despite his height advantage, his body's contours seemed to be a perfect match to hers. Joy had once read that people were all the same height when horizontal. Why she thought of that now, she wasn't sure. Or, maybe she was. Thinking about height was easier than thinking about the rightness in the feel of him. There was a sense of coming home. It was every dream she'd ever had, every fantasy she'd ever indulged.

"Daddy, you're smooshing Joy," Sophie said between giggles.

Joy rejoined reality with a thud that more than matched their fall. "Get off me, you fool."

"I don't think I can move." Whatever she had thought she'd seen was replaced by Gabriel's chuckles. He climbed off her and slipped again, this time landing thankfully on the creek bottom, not on her.

Joy climbed damply out of the water and watched as Gabriel and Sophie played in the creek's shallows. She was going to miss them more than she ever would have imagined possible.

"Lunch," she called when watching them became almost too painful to bear.

As if the significance of this picnic hit them all, they ate in silence. After they finished, Sophie curled up on the blanket and dozed.

"Joy?" Gabriel whispered.

"Shh. Sophie's sleeping." Joy slid across the blanket, putting some distance between herself and Gabriel. Distance. That's exactly what she needed. Tomorrow, she'd have all the distance she needed, she thought glumly.

"Good."

"Good?" He was looking at her. Oh, people looked at people all the time, but not like this. There was an intensity in his gaze that made Joy nervous. Very nervous. She wadded up the sandwich bags.

"Joy," he said, his big hands stilling hers. "Do you know what I've wanted to do since we fell in the pond?" He stopped. "No, I take that back. Do you know what I've wanted to do for longer than that?"

"What?" It was a foolish question. Joy could see what he wanted. He was going to kiss her. And most foolish of all, Joy was going to let him. She was leaving in the morning, and one last time she wanted to feel Gabriel's lips on hers. She wanted to capture a piece of him and hold onto it tight.

"Come here and let me show you." Cautiously, Joy moved closer.

She looked nervous, and Gabriel could sympathize, because he was nervous, too. This small woman was dangerous to him. For a comfortable woman, there were times that Joy was decidedly uncomfortable, and this was one of them.

Tentatively, he reached out and stroked her cheek with his fingertip.

"Gabriel?" she whispered.

"I'm going to kiss you. You know that, don't you."
She nodded.

Not exactly the most enthusiastic invitation, but it was enough for him. He wrapped her in his arms, once again overwhelmed by the sense of rightness. This woman belonged in his arms.

But she was leaving tomorrow.

The thought was an unwelcome intruder. As his lips finally met hers, he realized he didn't want her to leave the next day. He didn't want her to leave at all. Holding Joy, kissing her...it felt right. She belonged with him and Sophie. They needed her, and Gabriel suspected that she needed them as well.

He deepened the kiss, claiming her. He didn't want Joy to leave, and he was going to do his damdest to keep her from going anywhere.

"Daddy, why are you kissing Joy?"

Joy and Gabriel jerked apart. "I—"

Before he could form a coherent answer, Joy said, "Your daddy was just giving me a goodbye kiss."

"Oh."

Sophie's sad response tore at Gabriel's heart. There was no way Joy could leave. They needed her. He had to make her understand. He'd been thinking about it since last night and had finally come up with an idea. A brilliant idea. He was going to tempt her with the most precious thing he owned. Hopefully, it would be enough to keep her here. And he wanted her here—here with him, here with Sophie. It's where Joy belonged.

Now, if only he could convince Joy.

***

An hour later, the three soggy slime skaters plodded into the house.

"To the shower," Joy commanded the littlest, least slimy skater.

"That was fun," Sophie said. "And I liked pickles on my peanut butter and jelly."

"Me too." Joy's secret peanut butter and jelly ingredient used to gross her family out, but she figured a kindred six-year-old would enjoy it.

"Yuck," Gabriel said.

"He's got no taste," Joy told Sophie.

"Yeah, he's an old fogey," Sophie said. She squealed and bolted up the stairs when Gabriel made a face and lurched toward her.

"Thanks for a wonderful day," Joy said. "I'm going to de-slime and then get the truck packed so all I have to do is hop in tomorrow morning."

"We'll miss you," Gabriel said softly. "Sophie's going to be lost without you."

"I'll miss being here," she admitted as she fled up the stairs before Gabriel could say anything more.

She was going to more than miss them. Joy was afraid leaving the St. Johns would leave a permanent hole in her heart. She put the thoughts and the empty feeling out of her mind as she emptied drawers into her bag.

Gabriel knocked softly on her open door, and stood there, filling the frame. "Joy, I wanted to talk to you."

"About?"

"You know Sophie's going to be devastated without you here. What am I going to do with a six-year-old who's pining for her kindred spirit before she's even gone?"

"I've got to get back to work. I've been thinking about that trip to Alaska. Maybe it's time I took it."

A scream shattered the silence. "No!"

Sophie hurtled into the room, wrapped in her bathrobe. "No, you can't go to Alaska! I won't let you!" she screamed, throwing herself into Joy's arms.

Using her sternest voice, Joy said, "That's enough out of you, young lady. First off, this was a grownup discussion and you were eavesdropping, which is rude. Secondly, I have an important job to do, and though I love you, I have people who count on me. If that means I'm going to Alaska, then so be it."

Joy felt the child convulse as she clung to her. "Please don't leave me," Sophie whispered.

"Well, I'm not leaving tonight." She untangled Sophie's arms from around her neck and gave her a push towards the hall.

She watched her walk slowly toward her room. "Joy," Gabriel said.

"I'm sorry, Gabriel. I didn't mean to hurt her. You have to believe me, that was never my intention."

"I'd like a chance to talk to you," he glanced at the stairs, "without any interruptions. I've come up with a solution to our problem."

"And what did you decide?" Joy asked, afraid of the answer.

"I decided marriage is the only answer."

"You what?" Joy asked, sure that she'd heard him wrong.

"Let me get Sophie tucked in, and then we'll talk," he said.

How like a man to drop a bomb and then leave her to stew in it.

The three fairies popped into the room.

Blossom, with her neon hair, was always shining, but now she was positively radiating as she twirled around in what could only be the brightest yellow bridesmaid dress in history. "See, he wants to marry you."

"No," Joy whispered. "Not me." Could he be talking about them? Joy Aaronson St. John. It had a certain ring.

Sternly she shook her head. No, he meant Helen. He and Helen had decided to get married. That would solve a lot of Sophie's problems. She'd see that Helen was there to stay, and she'd have to accept it.

"Helen. He's going to marry Helen." Gabriel wanted to tell her himself that he was marrying Helen. Maybe he felt guilty about those few stolen kisses. Thinking about them made Joy's heart flutter. She pushed the feeling aside. She wasn't the type to win a man away from a beautiful woman.

"That's not what he said," Fern argued.

"And what about those kisses?" Blossom put her hand over her heart and looked as if she was going to swoon.

"What kisses?" Joy tried to act innocent, and goodness knew she was still innocent where Gabriel was concerned, even though she might wish she wasn't.

Myrtle looked far too pleased with herself. Her gown was a much more elegant affair, but almost scary in a blood-red sort of way. "You know what kisses."

"You were spying?" Joy was going to have it out with Grace. How could she have released such menaces on an unsuspecting world?

"We don't spy," Fern huffed. She avoided eye contact with Joy and fussed with the huge moss-green bow on her gown.

"Well, not really spying," Blossom hedged. "You've read the books, and you know that we can read your mind."

"You spied."

"It wasn't spying." Myrtle's eyes didn't quite meet Joy's. "We're your godmothers, and we just know these kinds of things."

"And he did kiss you, and you did like it." Blossom obviously had no problem living with the guilt of spying. She still appeared ready to swoon at the idea of Gabriel and Joy kissing.

Those kisses had been nothing but hormonal urges. Gabriel was a healthy adult male—she was a healthy adult female. They'd been thrown together, and instinct had taken over. Yes, that's what it was.

"Go away," she whispered to the fairies before she went down the stairs with her briefcase. She'd set up a surrogate office on a corner of the table. She began stacking the papers in her case, but her mind wasn't on packing. It was on kissing.

Joy would have to reassure Gabriel that she'd never seen those kisses as anything more than what they were—brief, hormone-induced mistakes. She would let him see that she was happy for him and Helen.

Her mind raced in circles. She hoped he would consider allowing her to stay a part of Sophie's life, but she wasn't really worried. She knew Gabriel well enough by now to realize he wouldn't keep Sophie away from someone she loved. But Joy would have to back off and allow Sophie to bond with Helen. However, as newlyweds, he and Helen would probably enjoy the time alone, so maybe she could still see Sophie.

Thinking about what Gabriel and Helen would be doing with that time to themselves caused a ripple of pain in Joy's chest, but she ignored that as well. She was happy for them. She forced a smile onto her face. Damn happy.

But not so happy to see the fairies had beaten her downstairs and were sitting on the island between the kitchen and living area.

Joy's heart sank. Though she hadn't really expected them to listen, she'd hoped that just once they would. "I told you three to go away."

"We weren't done talking about kissing."

"Well, you three don't know anything," Joy whispered. "There's not going to be anymore kissing. Gabriel's going to marry Helen. That will solve all his problems. He's probably planning to tell me to distance myself a bit from Sophie. It's obvious she's too attached. She'll need to bond with Helen."

"How can a little girl be too attached to someone who loves her?" Myrtle asked.

Joy had no answer for that question, and she was saved from trying to come up with something by Gabriel's appearance on the stairs.

"She's down for the night, with a stern warning not to leave the house without permission." He walked around the island into the kitchen. "Would you like something to drink?"

"We don't approve of drinking," Fern warned.

"Though a soda would be fine," Blossom added. Suddenly, the three fairies all had a can in their hands. "Ah, it hits the spot."

"I'm fine," Joy said. She glared at the soda-swilling fairies, silently warning them to be quiet. Gabriel's announcement that he was going to marry Helen would be hard enough to bear without juggling the objects of her dementia with her unrequited love.

"We're not leaving, Joy, but we will be utterly silent. At least until you and Gabriel finish this business."

Joy sent a powerful, silent wish that they'd all go away.

"Not on your life," Blossom said, a bucket of popcorn appearing on her lap.

Fern reached for a handful of the popcorn. "This is too good a show to miss."

"Pay attention, Joy," Myrtle warned. "Gabriel's talking, and it could be important."

Joy caught the tail end of a sentence, "...our marriage." Gabriel had grabbed himself a soda and taken a seat on the couch. "So what do you think?"

Gabriel and Helen? The thought was like a knife through her heart, but Joy didn't say that. Instead she said, "I think it's a good idea, Gabriel."

"You do?" he sounded surprised.

"Sure. I mean, it would solve a lot of your problems with Sophie. She might not be very receptive at first—"

"You don't think so? I thought she'd be overjoyed."

Overjoyed? Joy didn't think that was the word she'd used, but if Gabriel did, she wasn't about to burst his bubble. "Well, maybe you're right. When are you planning the wedding?"

"I was hoping as soon as possible. I know there are a lot of things to be cleared up, what with work, Sophie and everything, but—"

"That shouldn't be as hard as you think. I mean, Sophie's in school all day."

"And with the internet and phone, I was hoping it would work," Gabriel said.

Why would Helen need the internet? Erie was less than a half hour away, even during rush hour. She'd be able to work and still help care for Sophie. Helen, Gabriel and Sophie. She could see the three of them in her mind's eye, and it drove a lance through her heart.

Ignore it, she commanded herself as she said, "I'm sure it will work."

"We can tell her about the wedding, then."

Nervously, Joy glanced at her fairy trio, and all three waved merrily. "I don't think that telling Sophie is my place."

"I'm sure she'd like to hear it from both of us," he insisted.

"Gabriel..." Joy started to protest. She let his name drift off, unsure what to say next.

He reached in his pocket and removed a box. He thrust it at Joy. "What do you think? It was my grandmother's."

Why was he doing this to her? Joy realized he thought of them as friends, but this was too much. He had no way of knowing how deeply Joy cared for him. "I..." she stuttered, not taking the box.

"Joy, please?" he said.

It wasn't in her to deny Gabriel anything, so she took the box. Slowly, she opened it. The ring was gold, and in the center there was a beautiful ruby.

The three fairies crowded behind the couch and looked over Joy's shoulder.

"Oh, it's lovely."

"Stunning."

"Just the ticket," they exclaimed all at once.

"The perfect color," Myrtle proclaimed.

Reverently, Joy touched the stone. She had pictured Helen as more of a diamond kind of woman. A big diamond. She looked at Gabriel, trying to think of something to say. "It's beautiful," she managed.

"Try it on," he said.

She shook her head and handed the box back to him. "I don't imagine Helen would appreciate that."

"Why would Helen care when I gave it to you?" he asked.

He was annoyed. Joy could see that on his face, though she wasn't sure why. "Gabriel, no woman wants another woman trying on her engagement ring. I'm sure Helen would prefer you see it on her finger."

"What are you talking about?" he bellowed.

"What are *you* talking about?" she countered.

"You think I'm talking about marrying Helen?" Slowly, as if speaking to Sophie, he said, "I'm talking about you and me getting married."

"You and who?" she repeated stupidly.

"You and him," Blossom said.

"We were right," Fern added.

"See, Joy. We told you this was going to work out. You've got a proposal." Myrtle patted her sisters on their backs.

"You and me," Gabriel repeated softly.

Joy sank back to the couch. "I think maybe you'd better start this all over again. You're talking about you and me doing what?"

Eight

There was a hint of a smile in Gabriel's eyes. "You and me getting married."

Joy shook her head. "You and Helen."

He shook his head right back at her. "No. You and me."

"But Helen's the woman you love."

"Love? Where did you get that?"

"Told you," Fern said.

Joy glared at the fairies, and they all made a "zipping the lips" motion. "You and Helen have been dating."

"We work together. She goes to business dinners occasionally, and I'll confess I've been known to let people think it's social. After Trudi, I wasn't ready to go back to the meat market. So, Helen was a sort of buffer for me. Thinking we were a couple kept women away. But I thought you knew that's all it was."

"How would I know? You went on a date with her, and you talked on the phone with her all the time—"

"About business."

"And, she babysat Sophie."

"I can't believe you thought Helen and I...I mean, I kissed you. What did you think that was about?"

"Hormones?"

"Joy, Helen helped me out because we're friends. Anything else, well, it just isn't there." He sat next to her and took her hand in his. "Helen and I are friends, but I'd never date someone I work with."

"You love her," Joy insisted, trying to keep the wall she'd built between them from dissolving.

He shook his head. "As a friend."

"Even with those kisses, I know you don't love me," she said, fighting for something to keep them separate—to keep her safe.

"I...*we* need you, Joy. There's been something between us right from the beginning, and I think we'll get along well together. I'd be a good husband, and Sophie would be overjoyed to have you as a step-mother."

"But you don't love me," she insisted. She needed him to admit it, even though she knew it would tear at her heart to hear it.

"We're friends. The short time you were here, you became a part of our lives. Sophie and I need you."

"So what you're asking for is a marriage of convenience?" she asked, needing to fully understand what he wanted. She'd say no, of course, but she'd hear him out.

"That's not how I would classify it. I mean, we're both adults, Joy. We get along well enough together. Sophie adores you. You're not old, but you're not getting any younger. Maybe it's time you start thinking about a family. I'd like more kids, if you would."

"Gabriel," she started, but he was on a roll and kept talking right over her.

"From what you said, Ripples isn't tied to Chicago. You could move your office to Erie. I'll donate space in my building for it. Hell, Joy, I'll pay for the move, employee expenses and all."

"Joy, give him a chance," Myrtle said, obviously unable to keep her lip zipped.

Take a chance on marrying a man who didn't love her? No. She tried to say the word, to tell him no, but he steamrolled over her.

"You said you were tired of the traveling, well, here's your chance. Stay with us. Be my wife and be Sophie's mother. Take over the business end of Ripples and let your assistant do most of the traveling."

"Gabriel, I don't think either of us would be doing the other any good marrying when we don't love each other." He looked like he was going to argue. She held up her hand, silencing him and then qualified, "At least not the way a husband and wife should."

"We'd be good together. I want you more than I remember wanting any woman." He paused, then added, "Sophie needs you."

Joy couldn't respond. If Gabriel had told her he loved her, that he wanted to marry her because he loved her—not because he needed her and wanted her—she would have been in his arms shouting, "YES!"

She loved him. The force of the feeling hit her hard.

Joy Aaronson loved Gabriel St. John.

Damn those fairies. They'd cast a spell on her.

Myrtle shook her head. "You know we can't do that. Love is a greater magic than even a fairy can possess."

"No," she whispered. Love. It was a dangerous word, and one she didn't relish. Love changed people, and Joy didn't want to be changed.

She had a challenging job she loved. Okay, the travel was getting a bit old, and she wouldn't mind settling down, but it wasn't a priority, and she didn't need to get married to do it. She was the boss, the head honcho at Ripples. If she wanted to be a desk jockey, then she'd be a desk jockey. She didn't need Gabriel to accomplish it.

But there was Sophie.

"Sophie needs you," Blossom whispered.

Sophie did need her, and Joy needed Sophie. Joy had loved her since they bumped into each other.

"Joy?" Gabriel said softly. "I could make you happy."

She shook her head. "No one is responsible for anyone else's happiness. I like you Gabriel."

"You love him," Blossom said.

"I *like* you a lot. And I truly adore Sophie, but I don't think I'm cut out for a marriage of convenience."

"Joy, we've lived together, and we've gotten along famously. We have similar tastes in music and enjoy the quiet. We both have strong family values, and we both love Sophie. Sophie adores you. I like you, but more than that, I respect you. I have never felt this comfortable with a woman."

"Comfortable?" Joy asked, her eyes narrowing.

"Yes, comfortable. With Trudi there was a lot of...well, upkeep. And the women I've dated after her liked to party and be seen. That's why I took Helen to so many functions. Going out with women wasn't taking Sophie to an indoor park, slime skating or bowling. It was a black tie affair. Caviar and champagne. Well, I'm more ice cream than caviar, and I think maybe you are, too."

"So, let's see if I have this straight. You want to marry me because Sophie likes me, and you find me *comfortable*?"

"I think Gabriel made a mistake there," Fern muttered. "Comfortable isn't a very romantic word."

"I don't think he meant comfortable like a pair of slippers, but comfortable like," Blossom paused a moment, apparently trying to think of a word, "Um, like a good fit?"

Gabriel was smiling and nodding as the three fairies tried to help him out of the hole he was digging. "We'd be perfect partners. And as for the physical side, well, I think we'll be a comfortable fit there as well. Sparks have been flying."

"See?" Fern cried. "Sparks. That's better than comfortable."

"So, I'm comfortable, low upkeep and there's enough chemistry that you could stand me in your bed?" Joy stood, shot a glare at the fairies, then pressed her hands to her chest while she fluttered her eyelashes. "Well, Gabriel, that's probably the most flattering proposal I've ever received. But I'm afraid, that despite your eloquence, I'm going to have to decline your offer." She turned and stomped across the room. "Tell Sophie I'm going to Max's, and I'll come back tomorrow," she yelled over her shoulder.

"You're breaking your promise," Fern cried.

"No, I'm delaying it," Joy hissed, stalking to her truck.

"Joy," Gabriel said, following her at her heels. "I don't know why you're so upset."

She wheeled around and shook her head. "I'm sure you

don't."

Gabriel knew he'd screwed up this proposal, and he wasn't sure how to unscrew it. "Just think about it, okay? I might not be good at putting it into words, but I think we could build something solid."

He knew Joy had to be able to see how good they'd be together. She was too perceptive not to see it.

"I don't need to think about it, Mr. St. John. But thanks for the offer." She turned, climbed into the truck and slammed the door. He could see her mouth working as she started the ignition. Gabriel watched her speed off.

Women. He'd never understand them.

He sighed, shut the door, climbed the stairs and opened Sophie's door. He replayed his proposal as he watched his daughter sleep. He was sure Sophie would be delighted if Joy came to live with them. Sophie would miss Joy if she left. Hell, so would he. Seeing her with Sophie had seemed so right.

Why couldn't Joy see it?

***

"The nerve," Joy muttered.

"He did say sparks." Blossom, wedged between Fern and Myrtle in the front of the truck, wasn't about to let the sparks go.

But as far as Joy was concerned, any sparks she'd felt had fizzled with one word. "Comfortable? I'm *comfortable*." She dodged a pothole. "Is that the kind of prince charming you'd find for a godchild? Charming? Ha! A prince that's able to settle for being *comfortable*?"

"That's not all he said," Fern argued.

"Sparks. Sparks are good," Blossom chimed.

"Girls," Myrtle silenced her sisters. "Now, Joy."

"Don't you *now Joy* me. He said comfortable. He wants to marry me for Sophie's sake." Joy wished she was on a highway, somewhere that she could put her pedal to the metal and relieve some of her frustrations with speed. Instead, she was moving at a snail's pace along Greene Township's dirt lanes. She played at missing potholes, but it wasn't nearly as satisfying as speed would be.

Or punching Gabriel St. John.

"The audacity of the man. He wants to marry me because I'm comfortable, and because I'm good with his daughter."

"Sparks!" Blossom shouted.

"Oh, he'll even condescend to make it more than just the marriage of convenience that it actually would be. Maybe there are enough sparks to get him into my bed and give me babies. After all, I'm not *getting any younger*." She missed dodging a particularly big pothole, and the entire truck rattled.

"But sparks are just tiny flames. I want to be married because of a forest fire, not something that needs to be fanned into life. I want a man who's unable to keep his hands off me, who's drooling with desire. More than that, I want someone who loves me on more than a physical level. I want it all."

"With a little fanning, those sparks could become that forest fire," Blossom said.

"I don't want to have to work that hard."

"Who ever said love was easy?" Myrtle pressed.

"Darn!" Joy swore as she didn't quite manage to avoid a Herculean-sized pothole. With the way her day was going, she'd probably end up being engulfed by a pothole and forced to wait for Gabriel to ride to the rescue.

"Oh, that would be romantic," Blossom cooed.

"Damn it, don't go prying into my thoughts!" Joy was an easy-going person, but she had reached her limit—her absolute limit.

"Sorry," Blossom whispered.

"Now see what you did, Joy?" Fern's voice was full of censure. "She's going to cry."

"No, I'm not," Blossom said.

Joy could hear the tears in Blossom's voice and felt a twinge of regret. "I'm sorry. It's just that I don't want to wait for any man to come to my rescue."

"That's what Grace said, too," Myrtle said.

"What's with women these days?" Fern asked. "It used to be all women wanted a white knight."

"It's the new millennium. If I sink into a pothole, I'll manage to get out by myself. I can change a flat tire. I know my way around engines. I don't need a man to ride to my automotive rescue."

"Everyone needs to be rescued sometimes," Fern said. "It seems to me that you could take turns."

"No. I don't need a man at all. Especially one who thinks I'm *comfortable*." She dodged another hole. "See? I don't need Gabriel."

"What about Sophie?" Myrtle asked softly.

"Okay, I might need her, but not enough to marry a man who doesn't love me."

"You'd love to be her step-mother," Myrtle pressed.

"But not at that price." Joy missed a small hole and the truck bounced.

"Marrying the man you love is such a heavy price to pay." Myrtle's voice was tinged with sarcasm.

"Oh, shut up!" Joy shouted. "No one likes sarcastic, mind-reading fairies butting into their love life."

"You don't have a love life," Fern pointed out.

"At least not yet," Blossom added merrily.

Marry a man she loved, one who didn't love her back? Marry a man who saw her as over-the-hill and comfortable? No matter what the fairies said, it was too high a price, despite her love for Sophie.

She dodged another pothole and was just congratulating herself on her driving abilities when a deer darted from the trees lining the road.

"Oh!" Joy shouted as she yanked hard on the steering wheel, missing the deer by inches and hitting a huge tree instead.

"Joy?" Three fairies stared at her.

She sat stunned for a few minutes and then moved slowly, assuring herself that she hadn't done any permanent damage to herself. Her left shoulder hurt where the seatbelt had cut into it, and her neck felt a little stiff, but she seemed to be in one piece. "I'm fine," she whispered. "Are you three all right?"

"We're fairies. We don't get hurt in car accidents."

Talk about a disaster waiting to happen. That's what Joy's mother had called her on more than one occasion. And, in this instance, Joy had to agree.

"No, Joy. It wasn't your fault," Blossom soothed.

"You're right. It's your fault. If you hadn't distracted me, I wouldn't have hit the tree."

"If you weren't so stubborn, we wouldn't be distracting you," Myrtle muttered.

"If you all stayed in Grace's books where you belong, I wouldn't have to be stubborn."

"Well, if you really paid attention, you wouldn't worry that he sees you as just comfortable." Myrtle offered Joy a hand. "You'd know he wants you."

Moving slowly, Joy climbed out of the truck. Country roads weren't notorious for their streetlights, and the glow the tiny sliver of moon provided barely relieved the inky blackness. Joy couldn't make out much about the truck, other than its front end seemed to have become fused with the gigantic tree. There was a hissing noise that didn't bode well. Both headlights were out, so even if she could get the truck to start—and listening to the hissing sound, she doubted she could—she wouldn't be able to maneuver on the dark roads.

Now what?

"Do you three fix cars?" she asked hopefully. If she had to have fairy godmothers, they might as well be of some use.

"No, we don't fix cars, we just fix hearts," Myrtle said.

"You're not doing a very good job of that. Maybe you could do a better one with my truck?"

"If you'd just cooperate," Fern said, frustration apparent in her tone, "you'd make the heart part easier. If you want the truck fixed, call a mechanic."

Useless. The fairies were utterly useless. "Do you at least have a phone?"

"No, we have your-own-true-love."

"Dammit, Fern. This isn't funny," Joy said.

"No, you're right, it's not," said Myrtle. "We'll just leave you to think about things on your way back to Gabriel's."

"I'm not going back there. I'll keep going down the road and call for help from someone else's house."

"No you won't." The three fairies blinked out of sight.

Damn the fairies. She wasn't going back to Gabriel's. Joy

reached into the backseat, picked up her purse, tossed it over her right shoulder, which wasn't aching, and started to walk in the opposite direction from which she'd come.

She was walking away from Gabriel and his comfortable marriage of convenience.

Half an hour later, she stood in front of Gabriel's driveway.

"I'm not going back," she called. The fairies didn't answer.

She started back up the road. There was a house at the corner, the one Sophie and she had passed on their way back from Max's. Half an hour later she stood in front of Gabriel's driveway again, though she'd headed away from it. There had been no house, just a tree-lined road.

"Does every road lead back to Gabriel's?" she called.

"For you they all do," came Myrtle's disembodied response.

Nine

"I won't do it," Joy maintained.

"Then you'll spend the night on the road," Myrtle's voice insisted.

Reconciled to the inevitable, Joy cursed as she plodded down the length of the driveway. Just because she was using Gabriel St. John's phone didn't mean she was going to marry him.

Her left shoulder still hurt from the accident, her right one throbbed from carrying her purse for so long. Her neck was getting stiffer and her head ached. But none of her injuries hurt nearly as much as her feet. She'd stumbled over rocks and into potholes so regularly, it had become a part of her cadence.

Step, step, stumble, trip, stumble, step, step. She'd actually done more than stumble twice. She'd fallen, and both knees hurt. She'd actually ripped a hole in her jeans during one fall.

"I thought you were supposed to protect your godchildren?" she called, but there was no fairy answer.

No surprise there. The three fairies seemed to have an uncanny knack for not being around when their godchildren truly needed them. They just showed up enough to cause trouble. And going back to Gabriel's house was trouble with a capital T. At least it was for Joy and her fragile heart.

She tried to force her thoughts from Gabriel and his absurd proposal. She was just too tired and too miserable to fret about it any longer. She wanted to sit down, regain her strength and then kill some fairies. She doubted a jury in the world would convict her.

She knocked quietly on the big wooden door, hoping she wouldn't disturb Sophie. For the most part the little girl slept like a log, but today, after all her excitement, Joy wasn't counting on it.

She knocked again, a little louder.

Apparently Gabriel slept as soundly as Sophie did.

She actively thumped on the door, wishing the man had thought to put in a doorbell. She waited, praying she'd hear the thud of steps or see a light switch on. Neither happened.

Now what?

"What have you all done now?" she asked. This time she didn't expect an answer. The vagaries of fairies. That was a great title for a book about these three. She'd have to mention it to Grace.

"Oh, we'll tell her. You're right. It would be a great title."

"Blossom!" If one of the fairies appearing made her feel relieved, Joy definitely was at the end of her emotional rope. But relief was just what the neon-yellow clad fairy's appearance made her feel. "Where are the other two?"

"I snuck back to help you." Blossom's windsuit wasn't nearly as bright as her smile. "Fern and Myrtle are kind of put out that you're ruining our plan by being so stubborn."

"Can you unlock the door?" Joy asked hopefully.

"No. That would be breaking and entering. A huge no-no in the fairy rule book."

"Can you wake Gabriel?"

"No. Sorry. Gabriel can't see me, remember?" She studied the porch a moment. "But, how about the window? I mean, there's no rule in the books about me *helping* you break and enter. Gabriel wouldn't mind, especially when he hears of your adventures."

"Maybe he'll give me a lift into town tomorrow. I can rent a car and send someone to pick up the remains of my truck. Unless the three of you could take care of it?"

"Sorry, dear. It's against the fairy rules."

"What I want to know is just what good are fairy godmothers?" She pushed the screen up. It didn't budge. Grunting, she pushed harder. "They can't fix cars, can't break and enter, and can't open windows." She gave up and whirled on Blossom. "There seem to be more can'ts than cans in that rule book of yours."

The fairy sniffed inelegantly. "We're pretty good at finding our godchildren the right true love."

"There's a problem there, too. My own true love just wants to marry me for his daughter's sake. Because I'm comfortable. Because he's not unattracted to me. And with my biological clock ticking, he figures we can make a baby or two before it explodes."

"It's a start," Blossom said. "And don't forget the sparks. He did say sparks."

"And I said I dreamed of a man who'd drool over me and fall madly in love with me."

"Oh, he'll be drooling over you before everything is done."

Softly, Joy asked the question that haunted her. "But will he ever love me?"

"Joy—"

"Never mind." It was time for Joy to put away her fairy tale version of true love. Maybe she should settle. After all, Blossom was right, Gabriel had said sparks. "I guess the way you three see it is beggars can't be choosy."

"Oh, Joy, I think—"

Joy cut her off. "We'll worry about my love life later. Right now I'm more concerned with getting inside and getting some help."

Ignoring Blossom, Joy tried to remember how the windows latched, but for the life of her she had no idea. She reached in her pocket and pulled out a quarter. Gently, she wedged it into the crack between the window frame and the screen. She levered it, trying to pop the screen outwards. It didn't move. There had to be some latch locking the screen in place.

"Now what?" Joy murmured. She ached all over, and she was pretty sure the knee underneath the torn jeans was bleeding. She could try the other windows, but it was too dark to see, and it was a pretty good bet that however this one latched, the rest did too.

She knocked on the door again, though she held little belief that it would prove successful. It didn't.

"You could curl up on the porch and wait until morning," Blossom said cheerfully. "Or..."

"Or?"

"You could climb up to Gabriel's window. The roof over the porch isn't all that high. You could use the little tree over there, and you should be able to get high enough to climb onto the roof."

"What if it's locked?"

"You bang on it loud enough to raise the dead."

"I think I'd rather bang on his thick skull than his window," Joy muttered.

"That's the spirit."

She was too tired to think of a better plan, though having read about Blossom's plans in Grace's books, Joy was pretty sure there had to be a better one. But since she couldn't think of it, she trudged to the small tree, resigned to her fate. She didn't have to climb too far, just high enough to boost herself onto the roof.

Ten minutes later, feeling her spirits rise slightly because of her totally awesome climbing abilities, Joy was on the roof and inching towards Gabriel's window.

"Did you see that, Blossom? I'm a goddess—a tree climbing, problem-solving, deer-sparing goddess." Patting herself on the back wasn't difficult at all, despite her aching shoulders. The end of her ordeal was at hand.

Blossom hadn't followed her. Chicken.

She reached the window. "Way to go Joy," she whispered. Talking to herself probably meant she was losing what little sanity she had left, though talking to herself was preferable to talking to fairies.

"Gabriel?" she called, rapping on the screen, which wasn't overly effective. "Come on Gabriel, I need you." How could the man sleep through the commotion she was causing. "Gabriel?"

Now what was she going to do?

She might have made it up the tree, but she doubted she'd make it down in the dark without breaking her neck. Suddenly, the absurdity of her situation struck her. She was stuck on a roof in the pitch black night, injured and cold, with little hope of rescue. It was all the fairies' fault. No, it was all Gabriel's fault. It had all started when he had asked her to marry him.

Joy giggled, a small tiny squeak that progressed into a full-fledged belly laugh. She was known for her ability to attract catastrophe, but this took the cake. Calamity Joy, her brothers used to call her, and in this instance, they hadn't been much off the mark.

Movement inside the house caught her eye. "Joy?" Gabriel's form was silhouetted in the window. He opened it, which left them separated only by the screen. "Joy, what the hell are you doing on my roof?" Through the screen she could see he was wearing boxer shorts and nothing else.

Joy's mouth went dry, but she forced herself not to let it show. She'd seen him in his boxer shorts that first day when she'd spilled coffee all over him. And it was too dark to make out much. She could handle the fluttering in her belly.

"I'm just admiring the night sky. That's the Big Dipper, isn't it?" she asked innocently.

Gabriel looked at her as if she'd lost her mind. Well, she probably had. "Ask a stupid question, get a stupid answer," she told him.

"You think asking what a woman is doing on my roof at," he glanced at the digital clock, "two sixteen in the morning is a stupid question?"

"I think a better question might be, *Joy, would you care to come in?*" She edged towards the window. The end of her ordeal was at hand, or rather at foot, since she was edging feet first. "Just open the screen, however the damn things open, and let me in."

"Are you going to marry me?" he asked out of the blue.

"What?" Of all the things she expected to hear him say, that wasn't one of them. "Gabriel, stop playing games and just open the window."

"Just tell me, are you going to marry me?"

"Gabriel." She was slipping. She was going to fall to a gory death all because of Blossom's absurd plan and Gabriel's warped sense of...what was it, humor?

"Gabriel, let me in." He just studied her. She'd have known he was looking even if the darkness that enveloped them was total. As it was, the slight illumination of the moon was enough for her to see his serious expression. There wasn't a hint of humor in it. Humor wasn't on her mind as she whispered, "Yes."

The word momentarily surprised her. There were a thousand reasons she should have said no, not the least of which was that saying yes was probably the dumbest thing she'd ever done. But there had never been anything Joy wanted to do more than to marry him.

The fairies had bumbled again. They'd found Joy her own true love, but they'd forgotten to make sure he loved her, too. For Sophie's sake, maybe she could learn to settle for half the prize.

"Yes?" his whisper echoed her own.

"Yes." Feeling vulnerable, and not because she was going to fall off the roof at any moment, she said, "Now let me in before we have to get married in the hospital. The paper can report, *The bride wore a beautiful white cast, accented by a stunning metal pulley system.*"

"Come on in, Joy."

"Why do I suddenly feel like a fly being beckoned into the spider's web?" she grumbled. She inched towards the window as Gabriel released the latches and lifted off the screen. He held out his hand. Reluctantly she took it and allowed him to guide her into his room. It was the only room in the house that she'd never entered.

"I..." Joy started saying, then stopped. She had no idea what to say. She tried to pull away from Gabriel's embrace, but he held her tight.

"We'll talk later about why you were sitting on my roof at two o'clock in the morning, but for right now, just tell me again, will you marry me?"

"I said yes, and I meant it. I'll marry you for all the reasons you pointed out. You and I are compatible. We both adore Sophie. And leaving her breaks my heart. I'll accept your

marriage of convenience. I'm sure we'll get along just fine."
Gabriel held her. The clock glowed two-two-two. Two twenty-two, that was the time that Joy had forever changed the course of her life, she thought as she allowed herself to be drawn into her future husband's arms.

"I think we should seal our bargain," he murmured.

"How do you suggest we do that?" she whispered, her lips almost touching his.

"Like this." His lips melded with hers until nothing at all stood between them. Gently he forced her lips to part and tenderly explored her.

"Joy," he whispered, taking a step towards the bed. "I want you."

Those words brought Joy back from the fog he'd cast over her. She pulled back, fighting his arms to get some distance between them. "I can't."

"Can't what?" he asked, moving after her.

Joy continued to back up, needing some space, needing to keep her head. "I can't go to bed with you. Not now, not after the wedding."

He froze. "What the hell are you talking about now?"

"Gabriel, you listed all the reasons we should get married, and what it boils down to is that I'm convenient. We get along. I'm comfortable. Sophie likes me—loves me even. I'm not getting any younger. Well, maybe you're right, maybe I'm not getting any younger, but I don't need the table scraps you want to throw my way. I'll marry you, but I'm not looking for a physical relationship. We'll just solidify the partnership we had before. Sophie will feel safe knowing she has the two of us, and she'll be fine. There's no reason to actually consummate this relationship."

"No reason?" Gabriel said, his voice rising.

"Sh," Joy whispered. "You'll wake up Sophie." It was a totally illogical statement, and she realized it. If all her knocking and climbing on roofs hadn't awakened her, nothing was going to. But she needed an excuse to get away from Gabriel.

He took a step towards her and she countered it, finally running out of space in the small bedroom. She was up against the open window with nowhere to go but back on the roof.

"Gabriel, what on Earth is the matter with you?"

"You think that what just passed between us is nothing. That's not enough of a reason for me to be upset?" He was right in front of her though he didn't touch her.

The fairies popped into view behind Gabriel. "You said yes?" Fern cried.

"But not to the sex," Blossom groused. "That's the fun part."

"He's drooling over you, just like you asked," Myrtle added.

"Drooling, without love, is just a bunch of spit," Joy murmured. The thought was a knife cutting at her heart, but she wouldn't tell him, wouldn't give him that kind of guilt to carry around. She might have lost her heart to him, but she wouldn't lose her pride as well.

"Drooling?" Gabriel asked.

Joy glared at the fairies. Gabriel was going to think she was nuts. "We don't love each other, and I don't think the, er, physical end of a relationship can be satisfying for either of us without it."

"Come on, Joy. You know you want to jump his bones," Blossom said.

"Blossom," the other two fairies gasped.

"What?" the yellow fairy asked innocently. "She does."

"There are reasons we should marry, but, like all marriages of convenience, there's no reason to force ourselves to become physical. It's business, pure and simple."

"That's it, Joy. Make the man admit he loves you first," Fern cheered.

"Force ourselves?" Gabriel took a step closer, an ominous look in his eyes.

Joy side-stepped, not wanting to touch him, knowing she wouldn't be able to say no again if they did. Gabriel's momentum carried him forward and since Joy had moved, he leaned into what should have been the window, but wasn't since it was still open. He slipped forward, his top half sprawling onto the porch roof.

"Gabriel!" she shouted, grabbing the waistband of his boxer

shorts.
"Slowly, he rose and pulled Joy's hand from his pants. "The next time you put your hand down there, I hope you're intending to take me for a fall, not save me from one."

"Gabriel," Joy gasped. She didn't know what else to say, so she said nothing.

"If this is what you want Joy, I'll accept it." He turned and walked to his bedroom door. "The guest room is yours until you decide differently."

With as much grace as she could muster, Joy walked out the door. The soft glow of a nightlight lit the hall. "Goodnight, Gabriel."

"Kiss him, kiss him," Blossom chanted until Fern nudged her. "Well, she wants to," she muttered.

"And Joy," Gabriel said.

She stopped. Maybe he was going to ask her to kiss him goodnight? Despite her principles, Joy knew it wouldn't take much to get her to comply.

"See, she wants to kiss him," Blossom said.

Instead of begging for a kiss, Gabriel said, "I still want to know what you were doing on my roof at two in the morning."

Joy's sigh was echoed by three fairy sighs, Blossom's the loudest of the lot. "I'll tell you the whole story tomorrow, Gabriel."

"Tomorrow then. We can tell Sophie about the wedding and discuss the when and where."

"Fine," she said as she limped down the hall. Her aches and pains were suddenly coming back full force. She'd take a shower and then crawl into bed. Maybe tomorrow when she woke up she'd discover this was all some cosmically horrible dream.

"This is not a dream," Myrtle promised.

"Joy, are you okay?" Gabriel's voice whispered down the hall.

"Fine. I'm just fine," she stage-whispered back. Even softer she added, "At least I'll be fine if the three of you leave me alone."

The three fairies immediately disappeared from view. "See

you in the morning, Joy."

In the morning. The fairies would be back, and she'd arrange a wedding to the man she loved but who didn't love her.

***

Gabriel passed Joy a steaming cup of coffee over the island that separated them. "I think I've found another advantage," she murmured.

"Another advantage?"

"Yes. As you listed out all the reasons I should marry you, you didn't mention your coffee. It would have to be very high on my list." She took a sip. "Very, very high."

Gabriel sat down across from her and smiled tentatively. He'd been watching her like a hawk since she had come downstairs. It was as if he was afraid she would disappear at any minute. It made Joy feel hunted.

"Coffee is a very big advantage," Fern said.

One minute she was alone with Gabriel, the next, three fairies lined the counter. Joy resisted the urge to groan, and tried to ignore her three uninvited guests.

Myrtle wagged a finger in Joy's direction. "You might not have consciously invited us, but as you read Grace's books, more than once you wished someone would help you find your own true love—"

"And here we are," Blossom added merrily. "And you've found the man of your dreams."

Fern took a huge gulp of her own coffee. "He's even proposed, and you accepted."

"A marriage of convenience," Joy grumbled, forgetting Gabriel for a moment.

Not being able to see their uninvited guests, Gabriel responded. "Don't you think it's time we talk about this? Maybe it would be wise to start with why you were on my roof in the dead of night."

"I didn't start on the roof. I had a small accident." Thanks to the fairies, she silently added.

"Hey, I got you in the house," Blossom said.

"And engaged," Fern added, patting her cohort on the shoulder.

Gabriel looked startled. "Why the hell didn't you say you were in an accident last night? Are you hurt?"

"Just a little stiffness and a scraped-up knee. And if you recall, we had other things on our minds last night."

"Joy had kissing on her mind," Blossom chortled.

An image of throttling interfering fairies flashed through Joy's mind.

"That's not nice," Blossom said.

"What happened?" Gabriel demanded.

"There was a deer," *and three fairies*, she thought glaring at her merry matchmakers, "and there was me hurtling right at it. I swerved and missed it, but I didn't manage to miss the tree. I think I did some major damage to the truck, but it was off the road and should be fine until I get hold of a tow truck."

"I don't give a damn about the truck. I think we should call the doctor and have you checked out, just in case." He was on his feet and at the phone, dialing.

"See, he cares," Fern said, doing a bit of a Blossom swoon.

"Gabriel, I'm not going to any doctor's. I'm fine. I had my seatbelt on, and the worst thing I suffered was a couple bruises from the strap."

"Let me see," he commanded, pulling at her t-shirt.

Joy smacked his hand away. "I most certainly will not. I checked them myself, and I'm fine."

He glared at her, but did take his seat. He took a huge gulp of coffee, tossing it back like it was a shot of something stronger. The look on his face suggested that he wished it was indeed something stronger.

"Now, as I was saying, I walked back here after the accident." Joy didn't mention she'd tried to walk anywhere but Gabriel's house, but thanks to fairy intervention couldn't.

"You're a very stubborn girl," Myrtle said.

Joy shot her another dangerous look. "But you didn't come to the door."

"I was sleeping." He glared at her, as if it was her fault he fell asleep.

"I figured. I also figured if I could get to your bedroom window, I could wake you up. I was exhausted and I ached all over."

"Ached? Damn it, Joy. I am calling the doctor." He was back on his feet, telephone in his hand.

"Oh, it's so romantic," Blossom swooned this time.

"Be quiet and let me deal with this," Joy said to the fairies. At Gabriel's startled look, she tried to cover her slip by adding, "Gabriel, I'm fine. Now, it's your turn to listen. Put that phone down and come here. I'm not marrying a man who's going to pine for another woman. I might sink to a certain level, but that's too low to expect me to go."

"What do you mean sink?" he growled.

Miraculously all three fairies remained quiet. "This isn't a love match." *At least on your part*, she silently added. "And I can accept that, but I won't marry a man who's in love with someone else, not even for Sophie."

"Who the hell am I in love with?"

"Helen." Just saying the name sent a jolt of pain through Joy's heart.

"Like hell I am. We've been over this. But I'll say it one last time—and I hope you're listening. Helen is a friend, and she was a convenient front to keep other women at bay."

"Are you sure she knows that?" Joy needed to know. "What will you do with her now?"

"I'm sure she knows that. As for what I'll do with her—she'll still work for me, still be a friend, but she won't need to pretend we're something we're not anymore."

"No, you'll have me running interference. So, Helen's no longer necessary. Just where does that leave me when I'm no longer necessary?" It hurt to ask, but Joy was afraid it would hurt even more to leave the words unsaid. She wanted to be completely candid with Gabriel. Well, candid about everything except her true feelings. Those would keep. "Where will I be when you and Sophie no longer need me?"

Ten

"Give him a chance," Fern began, but one look from Joy silenced her. And it must have been ferocious enough to silence the two fairies next to her on the counter as well.

"Joy, it's not like that with you," Gabriel protested.

"It was like that with Helen, and she was just convenient. Oh, wait, no I remember, I'm comfortable as well."

"Damn it Joy, why are you twisting everything I say?" he exploded, slamming his hand against the cupboard.

"I'm not twisting, I'm simply trying to understand what it is you want, Gabriel. Where you think I'm going to fit into your life. For instance, since you say you're doing this for Sophie." He looked like he was going to protest, so she held up her hand. "And because you care about me and my convenience and comfort level, where will we be when Sophie's old enough to move out of the house? I realize that's twelve years down the road and life doesn't offer any guarantees, but do you see us separating at that time? Or will we still be married?"

"I told you I wanted other children with you," he exclaimed.

"Actually, you told me I wasn't getting any younger, and we could think about having them, or something to that effect. That's not the same as wanting to have children with me."

Gabriel raked his fingers through his hair, frustration painted in his every gesture and expression. "Joy, I'm better with machines than people. Give me a computer and I can make it sing. But give me a simple proposal, and I can't do anything right. What I should have said was, of all the women I've ever met, I can't think of one—not one—I'd rather have children with."

Joy's heart gave a little lurch in her chest. Maybe there was hope here?

"There's always hope." Myrtle braved Joy's wrath by continuing, "Gabriel just needs time to realize what you mean to him."

"You're so good with Sophie that I know you'd be good with other children as well. After seeing how Trudi handled parenting, I want my future children to have a mother who will put them first. You've already done that with Sophie. I can only imagine how diligently you'll guard your own children."

Any hope died. Not only was she an old, convenient, comfortable sort of woman, now he was comparing her to a watchdog, ready, willing and able to defend some yet-unborn children.

But despite that, she was going to marry him. Maybe she'd known it since the fairies confessed that Gabriel was the man they had in mind for her. Or, maybe she'd known Gabriel St. John was the man for her the first time she saw him smile.

"You love him," Blossom said, voicing the thought Joy kept trying to avoid, but kept coming back to anyway.

"Don't lose hope," Myrtle added.

Hope, Joy thought. That was the only thing keeping her going. Let him think he was getting good, old, comfortable, reliable Joy. Once the ring was on her finger, she'd show him just how uncomfortable she could be.

***

Every little girl dreamed about her wedding, but in all Joy's dreams, never once did she dream about not only marrying a man who didn't love her but having three fairies in attendance. The week had sped by. Every day Joy had thought about calling off this farce. Every day she prayed Gabriel would say he loved her. Every day her emotions see-sawed back and forth between despair and hope.

Sophie was ecstatic, Gabriel was pensive, and Joy had decided the fairies had well and truly driven her crazy, because she had to be crazy to be going through with this.

She'd gone through the motions. She had Alice pack up her things and ship them to Erie, and she'd put Ripple's move into motion. Gabriel, true to his word, had cleared space for a small office.

And now she was here at the Courthouse. There was no turning back.

Judge Gerald Terry stood solemnly in front of them. "And, do you Delphina Joy Aaronson take this man to be your lawfully wedded husband?"

"What do you suppose his friends and family called him?" Blossom whispered in her ear. "Gerry? Gerry Terry. What a name."

"His parents must have had a real sense of humor. It's worse than Delphina Joy," Fern pointed out.

Joy couldn't see them. They were too afraid of Sophie seeing them to materialize, but that hadn't stopped them from coming to the wedding. They'd been prattling in her ear since she'd reached the court house with Gabriel and Sophie.

Judge Gerry Terry—the name was stuck in her head now—cleared his throat, and Gabriel nudged her.

"Pardon?" Joy asked, trying to keep from smiling over the man's absurd name.

"He wants to know if you'll take Gabriel?" Joy didn't have to see Myrtle to hear the exasperation in her voice.

"He asked, if you take me to be your husband. If you're done thinking it over, maybe you could give us your answer?" Gabriel said.

Gabriel was looking at her as if she was crazy. Maybe she was. Hearing fairies in her head wasn't the most sane thing Joy had ever done. Actually, this marriage wasn't all that sane, either.

She shook her head. She'd been thinking the most ridiculous thoughts all morning. It was probably her mind's defense system, taking her away from what was bothering her.

She looked at Gabriel's stern face and ached to reach out and caress it, but she wouldn't. Couldn't. Not yet. She couldn't touch him because it would lead to more touching...a kind of touching she couldn't have until he loved her.

And he would love her. The fairies had promised her her own true love and she wasn't settling for anything less than that. They weren't off the hook until he said the words.

"Yes," she said, smiling at him. She might not have Trudi's tall, willowy looks, but he liked her.

"He'll love you, honey. How could he not?" Blossom asked in her ear.

Joy wished she could ask the fairy if she was sure, but didn't want to appear any more sanity challenged than she already did.

"Is that a *Yes, I have an answer*, or is it a *Yes, I'll marry you*?" Gabriel asked, exasperation in his voice.

"Yes, I'll marry you." She forced her mind from Gerry Terry's name, from fairies, and from the problem of how to make Gabriel love her and tried to pay attention to the ceremony.

"*I do* is the traditional response," Gerry Terry scolded.

"Yes, I do take you to be my husband," she said. And yes, some day Gabriel would love her, she added silently.

"Then I now pronounce you man and wife. You may kiss the bride."

"Kiss her, Daddy," Sophie cheered.

"Joy?" Gabriel asked, aware of the fact Joy had avoided him as much as possible during the last week. He'd railroaded her into this marriage—he knew that. He'd been afraid she'd change her mind, and then where would Sophie be? And of course it was Sophie he was worried about. "Do you mind if I kiss you?"

Joy seemed to be considering her answer. Maybe the marriage was wrong. It wasn't the first time he'd had the thought. Gabriel had even thought of telling Joy to forget it, to go back to her life. But every time he tried to get the words out, she'd smile or laugh, and he knew that no matter how selfish it was, he was going to marry Joy Aaronson. No, St. John.

Joy St. John. He liked the sound.

Shyly, she nodded and stepped into his embrace. Afraid of scaring her, Gabriel moved slowly, tenderly fitting his lips to hers with an ease he'd never known with any other woman. It amazed him how well they fit together, and if Joy would quit insisting on her own room, he was sure they'd fit as well in bed. One way or another, he was going to convince her. As the kiss deepened and flames of passion lit inside him, Gabriel realized he'd better get that convincing done soon. "Wow," he murmured.

"*Wow* yourself," she said with a smile.

"We're going to be good together. I swear it Joy."

She gave him a funny look. "I think there's a chance that we will be, eventually."

"Eventually?"

She nodded, looking at him seriously. "Eventually."

Gabriel dealt with the judge and then joined his wife and daughter. *His wife.* It felt right. More right than anything he could remember.

"Well, ladies, how about a celebratory lunch?" he asked, anxious to take his newly formed family out on the town.

Sophie shook her head, her hair creating a red wave against her blue dress. "I can't, Daddy. I have plans."

"Plans?" He had planned on them being a family this weekend and had hoped Sophie would prove to be a buffer from any awkward feelings that surfaced. Maybe it was cowardly, but all was fair in love—marriage, he corrected himself—and war. "I don't remember hearing about any plans."

"Grace called this morning and asked Sophie to spend the night." Joy said. "I'm sorry, I should have mentioned it."

"CheChe's lonely and Uncle Max and Aunt Grace—" Sophie stopped short. "I can call them that now, can't I?"

Seeing his daughter holding Joy's hand twisted something in Gabriel's chest.

"Sure can, sweetie." Joy turned to Gabriel. "I hope you don't mind, but when they called this morning I just said yes without thinking."

Gabriel wasn't pleased, but as he looked into his daughter's chestnut eyes, he knew he didn't have much choice. "Sure. No problem."

Joy knelt down and hugged Sophie. "I had to tell my family, and I guess Max and Grace are as good a place to start as any. They'll be surprised."

She looked up at Gabriel and gave him a look that said that surprised wasn't the emotion she was worried about.

Sophie giggled. "Yep. Can I tell them?"

"If you like." Joy turned to Gabriel. "I would have preferred keeping it to ourselves a while longer, but I don't think that's going to be possible."

"And just when did you want to tell your family, Joy? You didn't want them at the ceremony, didn't want any celebration of our wedding. Why?" Thankfully Sophie was skipping ahead of them towards the car.

"You know why," she whispered.

"Why don't you tell me why?"

"Gabriel, we've been through this. What we have isn't a real marriage, just a sort of business agreement. I wouldn't feel right having a big celebration, or even marrying in a church."

He was silent after that, not because he didn't know what to say. He knew just what he planned to say and just what he planned to do about his wife—*his wife*. She might not think this was a *real* marriage, but she was about to find out just how real it was.

He might not know his new brother-in-law and his wife, but Gabriel already owed them. With Sophie spending the night, he could begin trying to convince Joy that what they had was more than a marriage of convenience.

***

"Max! Grace!" Sophie squealed as she shot from the car the moment it stopped.

Joy saw her brother and his wife come out onto the porch. Her stomach fluttered. Marrying Gabriel was one thing—telling her family about it was another thing entirely.

Well, Max would just have to get over being annoyed, since his wife had created the fairies who had started the whole thing.

When Max approached, he swept Joy into a bear hug. "Are you going to introduce me to your friend?"

"Her husband," Gabriel corrected.

Joy pulled away from Max's embrace and glared at her husband. "Gabriel," she said, censure in her voice.

"Husband?" Max asked, his stance reminiscent of a long-ago knight's as he stood ready to rush to the defense of the poor and helpless. The only problem was Joy wasn't a poor, defenseless heroine in need of rescuing.

"Husband, as of an hour ago," Gabriel added.

"And you didn't see fit to invite any of your family, or at least inform us you were getting married?" Max said, turning on his sister.

"It was a private thing. We wanted to keep it that way." The problem with having a brother was they never believed a sister could take care of herself. Having two was even worse.

"*You* wanted to keep it that way," Gabriel, her ever helpful husband, offered.

"You didn't want us there?" Max asked.

Joy spotted Grace walking down the drive, CheChe on her hip and Sophie clinging to her hand. "Help," she shouted, happy to have reinforcements.

Grace smiled. "Help with what?"

"Help calm my brother who seems to think he must defend my honor."

"Leave her honor alone," Grace said helpfully.

"She just got married and didn't see fit to invite us," Max informed his wife. "*She* wanted to keep it private." He sneered the last word, telling everyone just what he thought of Joy's privacy.

"If you'll recall, we didn't invite her to our wedding," Grace reminded him.

"That was different."

"Yes, it was." A secret smile passed between the two of them, and Joy felt a pang of envy. That's what she wanted with Gabriel. Secret smiles and small codes no one else could understand. She wanted the relationship her brother had found with Grace. Like her mother and father had as well.

"It's just everything happened so quickly, we decided to keep it between us. Maybe we'll have a huge party to celebrate and invite the whole family."

Max looked slightly appeased and Grace hugged her. "Now, I'm so glad we invited Sophie to spend the weekend. Those tickets to the Ice Capades couldn't have come at a better time.

You and Gabriel can go celebrate—" Max frowned at the word, but Grace just went on talking, "And enjoy a small honeymoon."

"Are you going on a real honeymoon?" Max asked Gabriel.

"As soon as Joy gets her business settled and things are back to normal, I thought the two of us would sneak away."

"Yeah, the two of you are awfully good at sneaking off," Max muttered.

"Max!" Joy and Grace scolded at the same instant.

"Can I call you Uncle Max now?" Sophie asked, obliviously unaware of any friction among the adults.

"I can't think of anything I'd like better, sweetheart," Max said, scooping Sophie into his arms and pulling one of her braids. "I've always wanted a niece, and I can't think of any little girl I'd rather have fill the position."

He turned towards Joy and glared. "Well, you two should take off. We won't expect you until late Sunday."

"Max, thanks," Joy said, hugging him in an attempt to mollify him. "Would you mind holding off saying anything to Nick, or Mom and Dad? I'll call them next week."

He just nodded and started off towards the house, Sophie still in his arms. Grace juggled CheChe to one side and gave Gabriel a hug. "Welcome to the family, Gabriel. It's sometimes a bit crazy, but I think you're going to fit in just fine."

"Are you saying that marrying Joy is going to make me as nuts as the rest of you are?" he asked, a hint of a smile playing across his face.

"I can almost guarantee it," Grace said with a wink. She waved and followed her husband and Sophie.

"Well," Joy said. "That went better than I'd hoped."

"That was better?" Gabriel asked, opening the car door and ushering her inside.

"Oh, much better. Max is prone to analyzing things to death. I was afraid he'd want us to go inside and have a seat on the couch while he tried to figure out why we didn't want to share our wedding with the family."

"And why didn't *we*?" Gabriel asked, as he took his seat behind the steering wheel.

"You know why we didn't. It's not as if this is a love match and we want them to share our joy. This is a business arrangement, and it seemed wrong to invite them to what amounted to our signing of the contract."

She sank back into her seat, wishing it had been different. Gabriel tore from the driveway, and a heavy silence filled the car as they made their way home.

***

"Gabriel, do you mind if I put my grandmother's china cupboard in the dining room?" Joy called. Spending her honeymoon night unpacking her things wasn't what Joy had always dreamed of, but nothing about this wedding day had been part of any of her dreams.

"I said, do whatever you want," came Gabriel's surly reply.

"I don't think this marriage is starting off on solid footing," she muttered.

Blossom appeared on the other side of the box Joy was unpacking. "I don't think he liked you calling this marriage a business arrangement, or insisting on separate bedrooms."

"But that's what it is. " Joy's things had been shipped to Gabriel's. Unpacking seemed preferable to brooding about a marriage that wasn't real.

"Drooling. You said you wanted him drooling."

"Maybe. But I decided I want love more, not just a marriage of convenience."

"Convenient. Are you so sure that's all this marriage is to Gabriel?" Blossom asked softly.

"For now." She pulled the last of her grandmother's linens from the box. They'd been packed in a closet at her apartment. Joy had never seen the need to unpack her grandmother's treasures since she basically had used the apartment as merely a place to sleep. But now, she hoped that she could build a real home with Gabriel and Sophie, and unpacking the lace tablecloths and china seemed right.

"Do you really think Gabriel and I are destined for a happily-ever-after?"

Joy hadn't meant to ask the question out loud. She didn't even mean to think the question, since the fairies weren't above mind reading. But it was the question that weighed most on her mind.

Blossom answered, "We're your godmothers. Our job is to see to it. Getting you married was only half the battle. Getting you happy is the rest of it."

"Tell me which box you need," Gabriel called from the living room.

"The one marked china. Hang on, I'll help you." She'd had the movers put the cupboard in the dining room, but most of the boxes still lined one living room wall.

"I've got it," Gabriel said. He was in the doorway, a large box in his arms.

"Let me help," Joy said, trying to take one side of it.

"I said, I've got it," Gabriel snapped and gave a little tug.

"Gabriel," she said, still clinging to her side.

Joy was so caught up in arguing about which one of them would carry the box, that she failed to remember Blossom was in the room.

And Blossom was their downfall.

Literally.

Gabriel, Joy and the box, went tumbling over Blossom. The sound of breaking china reverberated in the quiet house.

"Oh, my," Blossom said. "Honey are you okay?"

"Joy, are you okay?" Gabriel asked. He stood and looked from Joy to the box.

"I'm fine." Joy surveyed the damage. "I have a feeling I'm in better shape than the china," she said to both Gabriel and the fairy godmother.

"Oh, honey, I'm so sorry. I know this was your grandmother's and it's all you have of her things." Blossom patted Joy's shoulder.

Fairy godmothers might be invisible, but they weren't without substance.

Gabriel put his hand on her other shoulder. "Joy, I'm so sorry."

"Never mind," she said to both of them. She shrugged out of their grasp. "It was only some old dishes and cups. I'll go through the box and see if anything's salvageable." She remembered the tea parties she'd had with her grandmother when she was little. She'd always been allowed to pour the tea from the big, hideously ugly teapot.

"Joy," Gabriel said and then stopped, as if he didn't quite know what to say.

"Would you mind carrying those boxes of books up to my room? The movers put the shelves up there, but they didn't get all the boxes upstairs."

She wanted to cry, and though she wouldn't allow a full fledged cry-fest, she needed at least a couple private sniffles as she searched the debris for survivors. Later, alone in her bedroom—her very lonely bedroom—she'd drain herself of tears.

"Okay," Gabriel said.

Joy was too caught up in all the emotions of the day to notice he had agreed much too easily. She opened the box, another casualty of her klutziness.

"This time it was my fault." Blossom's voice sounded as if she was on the verge of tears. "I should have gotten out of the way."

"No, it was me. Accidents and I are intimately acquainted. Look at my poor smooshed truck, or when I spilled the coffee on Gabriel, or—" She breathed out a sigh of relief when she removed the first few dishes, whole and complete. As she worked her way through the box, she found a tea cup with a broken handle.

"You can super glue it," Blossom offered.

Next came two salad plates that were shattered. No hope of salvage there. As she neared the middle she found the tea pot, an ugly monstrosity that represented so many happy memories, in pieces. Too many pieces for super glue to work its magic. Images of the past played before her eyes as she glanced at the shards.

Joy's eyes filled with tears, despite all her good intentions. It was her wedding day, a day for champagne and roses and...She smothered a sob. There was no champagne, no roses and no *and* in her future. She was married to a man who thought she was comfortable, and her grandmother's teapot was broken.

"Oh, Joy," Blossom murmured, holding her, rocking her.

Joy's sobs were muffled against Blossom's shoulder, but as they gained momentum she held herself in check. She didn't want Gabriel to hear her crying. It was bad enough Blossom knew.

She couldn't bear the thought of Gabriel feeling sorry for her. Though things were far from perfect, she knew that was the one thing—the one thing out of all the trials she was trying to hold up under—that she couldn't bear. It would be her undoing.

"Let me call the others."

"What?" Myrtle, a shower cap on her head and wearing a big white robe, asked. She surveyed the scene and said, "Blossom, what did you do?"

"They tripped over me, and Joy's grandmother's china got broken. But I don't think it's the china she's crying about."

"Of course it isn't." Fern was wearing a hunter-green riding habit and snapped the whip against her boot. "This isn't how a girl dreams about spending her honeymoon, with a man who sees her as a convenience rather than as the woman he loves."

"You three set this up," Joy reminded them, a small hiccup punctuating the sentence. "Why couldn't you just find me someone who loved me?"

"We told you at the beginning that this was a troublesome case. Gabriel is the man for you. We're hoping in time that he'll learn to love you." Myrtle's soothing voice had the opposite affect on Joy.

"Hoping?" They were *hoping*? "I figured the three of you wouldn't find me a man to love who was never going to love me in return."

"We think he'll love you soon," Fern offered.

"Sparks," Blossom said, jumping on her sparking bandwagon again. "Don't forget the sparks. And comfortable isn't so bad."

"Bad?" Her heart suddenly felt more shattered than the teapot. "It's worse. Why don't the three of you just get out? I think you've made enough of a mess of things today."

"Joy, we really think things will work out," Myrtle offered.

"But you don't know."

"We're fairies and have a sense of things that could happen, but we're not omnipotent."

"Just go."

"Joy," Blossom started, but Myrtle cut her off.

"Let her be." The three fairies disappeared.

Joy was left with the task at hand. Somehow she made it through the box, finding more casualties as she neared the bottom. There was no use crying over broken china. Leaving the broken pieces in the box, she rose and started moving the pile of survivors up to the table.

"Joy," Gabriel said.

"What?" she asked without turning to face him.

His hand was on her should and gently her turned her. "Honey, I'm so sorry."

"For what?" she asked. She shrugged and tried to sound nonchalant. "It was an accident. I'm used to them."

"I'm sorry for the china, but I'm more sorry I got you into this mess. I used you. It's something I'm not proud of. You're good for Sophie and me, and I used that goodness to trap you. What I never asked myself is, are Sophie and I good for you?"

He pulled her into his arms, but Joy held herself stiff, unwilling to weaken her defenses, slim though they were.

"I'd like to be," he murmured into her hair. "I think I could be very good for you if you'd just let me. Don't hold me at arm's length, Joy."

"I'm not doing it to hurt you," she whispered against his chest. "I need to maintain some distance."

"I'm your husband now. You don't need to be distant from me."

Joy didn't know how to explain it to Gabriel when she hardly understood it herself. "Gabriel—"

"I need you, Joy. As selfish as it is, it's true. I don't think I've ever needed anyone as much as I need you."

That simple statement was her undoing. Maybe he wasn't declaring his undying love, but he needed her. It was enough...for now.

"See, we told you," the fairies said as they reappeared in the room.

"Go away," Joy muttered.

"Please, don't send me away," Gabriel whispered as he started to release her.

Joy embraced him, tilted her head and searched for his lips. When she found them, she poured all her frustration, all her longings...all her love into that one kiss.

"Wow," he whispered when they finally came up for air.

"Wow, yourself." The fairies were still standing behind Gabriel, grinning like crazy. Joy shooed them with her hand. Sporting thumbs up signs, they finally left.

Looking at Gabriel—the man she loved, the man she had married—any wall she'd hoped to build and maintain crumbled. And somehow it didn't bother her. Maybe it would later, but at that precise moment she wanted nothing at all standing between her and her husband.

"Are you sure that you want...I mean, you said you wanted to wait, and I will. But Joy, I want you—*need* you—more than you can know."

She broke free from his arms and saw the look of disappointment on his face. Rather than flee, she took his hand and led him towards the stairs. "I think it's time I truly became Mrs. Gabriel St. John."

"Are you sure?" he asked, dragging his heels.

Eleven

Joy turned around and smiled. "Are you trying to talk me out of it?"

Gabriel laughed, a husky, seductive laugh that made Joy's stomach flutter. "Honey, I might be slow on occasion, but I'm not stupid."

"Well, let's go see how slow you can be," she quipped, pulling him towards the stairs. "But we'll try for slow after we try for fast." She pulled harder, moving towards the bedroom and her fate, before she changed her mind. "Very, very fast."

Gabriel's laugh wasn't seductive this time, it was just plain wicked. When they reached the top of the stairs, he scooped her into his arms. "I think I can oblige."

"I'll hold you to it," she whispered.

He kicked open the bedroom door, and murmured, "You're so beautiful."

"I'm not." Joy knew she wasn't beautiful. Would he be comparing her to other, more fashionable women? She felt shy and slightly embarrassed.

She tried to disengage herself, but he would have none of it. He held fast and whispered, "Tonight I'm an expert on Joy, and let me tell you that you are the sweetest thing I've ever experienced." He kissed her then, and, at that moment, Joy felt truly beautiful, as if she finally was right where she belonged.

Being with Gabriel, Joy found out what true joy was.

***

Awkward.

Joy was the survivor of many mishaps and had felt awkward countless times in the past, but never more so than she did lying in bed next to Gabriel the next morning. He hadn't moved, but Joy hadn't, either. She lay there, trying to understand how she'd ended up in Gabriel St. John's bed. It wasn't where she had intended to be, at least not until he loved her.

And yet, Gabriel's bed was exactly where she was. She couldn't imagine being anywhere else. She loved him. There were so many things to work out in their relationship, but the one thing that Joy was absolutely sure of was that she loved him. Being with him last night had been a natural outgrowth of that love.

"You're awfully quiet," Gabriel said. He rolled to his side so he was facing her.

"Good morning," Joy said, hiking the covers a bit higher.

"So, what deep thoughts have you been thinking so early in the morning?" His hand reached out and toyed with a stray piece of her hair.

She shivered and managed to stutter, "I...I...don't know what you mean."

His hand left her hair and trailed down her cheek. "You've been lying here awake for the last half hour, and I don't think you were thinking happy thoughts."

"Gabriel..." She didn't know what to say. In all honestly, she wanted him to tell her that what she'd done wasn't a mistake. If she couldn't hear the three words she longed to hear, then she would settle for hearing some words of comfort at least.

As if he had the fairy godmothers' ability to read her thoughts, he pulled her into his arms and murmured, "Last night was right, if that's what you were worrying about."

"Gabriel, all the reasons I had for not wanting this side of our relationship to develop are still valid."

"Joy, we were meant to be together, meant to be here in each other's arms this morning."

"I'm afraid," Joy whispered.

"Of me?"

She wanted to say she was afraid the fairies were wrong and Gabriel would never learn to love her. But she settled for saying, "Of everything. It's all happening fast. I don't think I can keep my head above water. And I need to keep my head because if I slip I'm going to drown."

"Honey, I won't let that happen. We need you, Sophie and I. Maybe I was selfish rushing you into this marriage, but I truly think that Sophie and I might fill some need in you, too."

Joy knew he was right. She needed them even more than they needed her. She just wasn't ready to tell him how deep that need went. There was so much she could tell him, so many words to be said. But she was afraid. Afraid to tell him that she loved him, afraid of his reaction. Worse than rejection would be his sympathy. Having Gabriel pity her would be too much to bear.

Joy filled a need in Gabriel and Sophie's life. She was his wife, and she was wrapped in his arms. What Gabriel had given her was more than she'd ever thought to hold. She'd save her worries for later when she was alone. For now, she just wanted to be with him.

"Gabriel," she said, wrapping her arms around him as well. "How do you feel about making love in the morning?"

Gabriel chuckled. "I think you can guess the answer all by yourself."

The feelings building within him had nothing to do with sex. They were too big and too new to properly analyze, but holding Joy, teasing her, being married to her felt...right. He looked at the woman he was married to. How on Earth had he gotten so lucky. Like magic, this woman had appeared in his life and become as much a part of him as breathing was.

He needed Joy. Gently, he stroked her hair. He needed her so much.

"Well, if I asked you sweetly, do you think we could give it a try?"

"I like the way your mind works, Mrs. St. John. I like the way other things work as well." God, he wanted this woman. Not just sex. He wanted to be more than the man she was married to, more than Sophie's father. He wanted to be her heart and soul. He wanted her to be his heart and soul.

He wanted her to love him, because...because...

The feelings that had been growing stronger since the moment he'd met Joy suddenly made sense. He loved her!

Before he could analyze it and try to decide how Joy would react to hearing those words, she said, "And I like the way your...well, the way you work, Mr. St. John," she assured him with mock seriousness.

Gabriel turned to his wife—to the woman he loved. "Well, let's see if I can make it work first thing in the morning."

He'd make love to her now, and he'd find a way to tell her he loved her soon. And then he'd find a way to make her love him back.

***

Two days later, Joy looked around the house as she took Sophie's hand to lead her up to bed. The house bore her touch now. Her family pictures stood beside a picture of Sophie and Gabriel on the mantle. What was left of her china lined the cabinet in the dining room. Her grandmother's quilt and rack were neatly tucked in a corner.

Gabriel's home was now her home, too. The thought was satisfying.

She climbed the stairs, passing what had been her room, on the way to Sophie's. Just as she shared a life and a home with Gabriel, she now shared his room. Her clothes hung next to his, and her personal items were intermingled with his. Part of her was thrilled at the thought of spending every night in his arms. Another part was afraid. She'd lost her heart to Sophie, who was so very easy and safe to love. She'd lost her heart to Gabriel as well. Joy very much feared that loving Gabriel wasn't going to be safe at all.

Sophie climbed onto her bed and looked at Joy expectantly. Joy hugged her and asked, "Are you sure you don't mind that I married your daddy?" She needed some reassurance that she'd done the right thing, even if the reassurances came from a six-year-old.

Sophie nodded and squeezed Joy tightly. "You'll tuck me in every night?"

"Well, there might be nights that I have to go somewhere, and every now and then I'll still have to travel for Ripples, but not too often," she hastened to add. "Other than those few times, yes, I'll tuck you in every night."

"And read to me?" Joy nodded. "And do the voices?"

Joy cackled a wicked cackle and said in a scary voice, "You can be sure of that, my pretty." She let out a peel of rusty laughter.

Sophie's delight was evident in her laughter. "I love you, Joy, er, Mommy. I can call you that, can't I? I mean, I know you're not my real mother. I never called her Mommy. She didn't like it."

Joy smiled, fighting the pressure that was filling her eyes. "Well, since you never called her Mommy, I'm pleased to claim that name. And I love you too." Feeling tears fighting to break free, and knowing she'd never stop the flow if they started, Joy said, "Now, I thought we'd start one of my all-time favorite books."

Joy went to Sophie's shelves. "*The Lion, the Witch and the Wardrobe*, by C.S. Lewis. You'll love it. There's a scary sort of witch and," Joy roared, "a wonderfully huge lion."

"I'd like that," Sophie said, snuggling into Joy's arms.

Gabriel watched his wife and daughter through the crack in the door. His wife. He liked the sound of that. His love. He liked the sound of that even better.

How had he gotten so lucky? He still couldn't figure it out. For two days he'd examined his feelings for Joy and tried to tell her. But he couldn't get the words out. What if she didn't love him back?

Once upon a time he had thought he loved Trudi, but whatever it had been hadn't been love. And Trudi had never loved him. Could he survive not having Joy love him in return? She cared about him, maybe even loved him as a friend, but he wanted more.

He wanted Joy to be as head-over-heels as he was.

Joy was so full of life, so full of love. It showed in the way she took care of Sophie. It showed in the way she saved Jay, the cat. Even in Ripples. He'd done some checking into the business Joy had started and managed to keep running on its shoestring budget. Her capacity to love shone brightly there as well.

She'd once said something about not fitting into her family. Max was a psychiatrist, Nick an attorney, and somehow Joy seemed to feel that what she did was less. How was it she couldn't see just how rare her ability to love was?

Gabriel left his *wife* and daughter reading, voices included, and walked down the stairs. Somehow, he was going to show Joy that what she had, what she did, was worth more than all the attorneys and head shrinkers in the world. She was worth more than she suspected.

In the past Gabriel had worked very hard to care for the women in his life. They were high upkeep, not just with the things they expected of him, but in the amount of energy he had to expend to love them.

Until Joy.

She was comfortable. So comfortable, in fact, that when he wasn't looking she'd crept right into his heart. He didn't have to think about it. He didn't have to work at it. It simply was there—he loved Joy.

But the thought of telling Joy he loved her was very uncomfortable. She'd married him because of Sophie. She liked him, even cared for him—it wasn't in Joy not to care about everyone. But love? She'd never mentioned the words.

She'd tried to keep their relationship from becoming physical. She kept emphasizing that she'd married him because of Sophie. She liked him, but she loved his daughter.

Well, Gabriel would see to it that changed.

How did a man convince a woman she loved him?

He'd woo her, much like heroes of old. Somehow he didn't think flowers and candy were the way to Joy's heart. He might not have a clue how to go about getting Joy to love him, but one way or another, he'd accomplish it. He had to.

"Gabriel?"

He turned toward Joy. "Sophie in bed?" he asked, as if it were any other night. But he couldn't stop smiling because it was anything but a normal night.

He loved her! For two days the thought kept exploding in his mind.

"She's had her story and is waiting for you to kiss her

goodnight."

"And after I've kissed her goodnight, do you think there's a chance I can kiss her storyteller?"

"Goodnight?"

Gabriel shook his head. "No, if I start kissing that particular storyteller, I have a feeling it will be a long time before we say goodnight."

Shyly, Joy nodded. "I think I'd like that."

"And Joy?" She looked at him, her eyes glowing, fueling the flames burning in Gabriel's heart. "Would you do the voices for me, too? I love the one you use when you shout as you—"

"Gabriel!" she cried, looking shocked, much to his delight.

"Oh, if it gets too loud, I can toss a pillow over your head so it doesn't wake Sophie."

"Gabriel!" she cried again.

Gabriel stopped teasing and followed the woman he loved upstairs. He'd tell her how he felt about her soon, but first he was going to do his damndest to see she felt the same way.

He loved her.

***

She loved him.

The thought kept intruding in Joy's thoughts as she showered, readying herself for Gabriel's *goodnight kiss*.

"See, I told you things would work out," Blossom called from outside the shower curtain.

"Do you mind? I'm in the shower." The last thing Joy wanted on this wonderful evening was more fairy help. Gabriel might not love her—yet—but he'd proved that he was right about them being physically compatible. Very, very compatible.

"The rest will come in time," Myrtle assured her.

Joy supposed she should be glad they were on the other side of the shower curtain. It was obvious they weren't going to allow her to finish her shower in peace. "I've decided to take it one day at a time. We've got time to work things out." Starting tonight.

"Joy, you've also got company," Fern called merrily. "Someone's knocking at the door!"

A little too merrily for Joy. "Pass me a towel." She turned

off the water and stuck her hand through the curtain. Wrapped in the terry cloth, she opened the curtain and peered suspiciously at the three fairies. There was another loud thump, loud enough that she could hear it all the way upstairs. "What have you three done now?"

"The door." Myrtle reminded her.

"Gabriel, someone's at the door. Can you get that?" Joy called. She eyed the three godmothers—it wasn't just Fern who was excited about something. All three looked as if they were ready to burst.

Who could be here that would put the fairies in such good moods? She leaned forward and wrapped her dripping hair in a second towel Fern had handed her.

"Get what?" Gabriel hollered from the bedroom.

"The door."

The bathroom door flew open. "Okay, I got the door. Is there anything else you'd like me to get? Maybe you?"

Joy couldn't resist smiling. She'd love to let Gabriel get her, but three fairies grinning with Cheshire-cat smiles meant trouble, and trouble meant it might be a while before she and her husband got to the *getting*. "Gabriel, someone's knocking on the front door. Downstairs."

"Uh huh." He stared at her.

"He likes what he sees," Blossom said in her swooniest voice.

"Why, he's practically drooling," Fern added merrily.

"See, we did make your wish come true," Blossom added. "Drooling and sparks. It doesn't get much better than that."

"I'm still naked, can you get it?" she tried again. The look in his eyes made her want to forget their uninvited guests at the door—and her unwanted guests in the bathroom.

Gabriel's grin broadened. "You're still naked, and I'd much rather get you than the door."

"Maybe I'll get naked again later and let you get me." *After the fairies had left*, she added mentally.

"But for now, why don't you get the door?"

"Party pooper," Gabriel said as he left.

"Here," Fern said, handing Joy a robe. "You're going to need it."

"I'm sure Gabriel will get rid of whoever it is."

"I wouldn't be so sure." There was an ominous tone to Myrtle's voice.

"What did you three do now?"

"It wasn't us," Blossom assured her.

"Well, not really," Myrtle amended.

Joy grabbed the robe and hurriedly put it on. She knotted the belt as there was a knock on the bathroom door. "Yes?"

"Joy! Joy!" Sophie's cry came from outside the door.

Joy opened it and looked at the little girl. "You're supposed to be in bed, sweetheart."

"I can't sleep. My new Grandma and Grandpa are here."

Oh, no. Max must have told her parents. Joy had been meaning to call them, but didn't quite know how to tell them she'd married.

Trying to look upbeat, Joy took Sophie's hand. "Let's go say hello." She tried to force herself to sound normal. But normal was the last thing Joy had felt ever since Trudi's houseparty.

"Mom, Dad," Joy called as she walked down the stairs.

"Why does my new grandma have her foot on Daddy's throat?" Sophie asked nervously.

"Remember when I said I learned to fight dirty?" Joy asked, smiling at Sophie. "My mom taught me everything I know about it." She glared at her mother. "But, your new grandma should realize showing off a black belt by flipping her new son-in-law onto the ground, and then cutting off his oxygen supply is very poor form."

Joy momentarily turned from her mother to Sophie. "Why don't you run upstairs and let the grownups talk for a few minutes."

"Will Daddy be okay?"

"He'll be just fine," Joy promised. She waited until Sophie was back upstairs before she turned to face her family. "Mother!"

The minute Sophie left the room, the fairies popped into view. Joy's life was going from bad to worse.

"Your mom has a black belt in karate?" Fern said, sounding impressed. "I've often thought about taking lessons. It looks like a handy skill." She paused a moment, then added, "Plus I'd look fantastic in the outfit." Suddenly, she was wearing a green karate outfit. "See."

Joy tried to ignore the fairy trio, but it wasn't easy. They sat lined on the island separating the kitchen from the living area, watching the tableau unfold before them.

"Don't you worry about us, dear," Myrtle said. "We'll just sit over here and watch the show."

Her life was out of control. Fairies on the counter, her mother's foot on her marriage-of-convenience husband's neck, and a little girl cowering upstairs. Delphina Joy Aaronson St. John had had enough. "Mother!"

"He won't answer my question," Miriam Aaronson said by way of explanation. She was shorter than Joy but, unlike her daughter, there wasn't a soft feature about her. Her hair was blonde and cut in a pixie wedge that emphasized her blue eyes and prominent bone structure. "And when I finish with Gabriel I was going to ask how you were, but I can see for myself."

"And how is that, Mother?" Joy asked softly.

"You're glowing. You love him don't you?"

Miriam watched her like a hawk while Joseph Aaronson, who had said nothing up to that point, studied her from his vantage point on the couch. Three fairies, still lining the counter, stared at her, waiting for an answer. Most disconcerting of all, Gabriel from his uncomfortable position on the floor under Miriam's sneaker, was watching her.

"Come on, Joy. It's time to 'fess up," Fern said.

"Say the words, Joy," Myrtle scolded.

"You know you want to. You love him. Say it," Blossom said.

"You do love him, don't you?" Miriam prompted.

Joy wanted to crawl in a hole and die. How could her mother do this to her?

"Answer her question," Gabriel said, his voice sounding a bit reedy what with Miriam's attempt to cut off his oxygen and all.

"Let him up, Mother," Joy said, stalling.

"Not until you answer my question."

"Yeah, answer the question," the three fairies cheered in unison.

Joy had always thought her mother was the most stubborn, aggravating woman she'd ever met, but the three fairies were even more aggravating.

"And stubborn," Blossom said merrily. "But, we suspect there's more of your mother in you than you'd like to admit. You're being just as stubborn. Tell Gabriel how you feel. Say the words, Joy."

She rolled her eyes and said, as calmly as she could, "Mother, what Gabriel and I have is between Gabriel and me. I don't care what Max told you, and don't bother denying he told you something. Max ran behind my back and tattled, or you wouldn't be here. But it's none of his business, just like it's none of yours. I've never pried into your relationship with Daddy."

"Your mother and I love each other and had our share of prying at the start," Joseph said quietly.

"Daddy, you're supposed to be on my side when she gets like this." Joseph might not say much, but he generally could be counted on to try to control the worst of Miriam's temper.

He just shrugged. "Sorry, honey, but I want to know, too. Max said something about this being a marriage of convenience. That's what set your mom off. Her tactics might not be very diplomatic, but they tend to get results."

Miriam nodded, her arms folded, her foot still pinning Gabriel by his neck. "This whole thing sounds much too suspicious to me. I want to make sure you married for the right reasons."

"And what would that be?" Joy said, still stalling.

"Love. Marriage is hard enough if you love each other. It's next to impossible without that for a foundation."

"Answer her question, Joy," Gabriel said.

"Answer your mother's question, Joy," the fairies said in unison.

Joy looked helplessly around the room. Her mother, her father, and Gabriel all waited expectantly for her answer. The three fairies were literally sitting on the edge of the counter.

"Fine. I love him, for all the good it does me. And you might as well let him up right now because I can give you his answer. He married me because I'm old and comfortable, sort of like a pair of bedroom slippers. He tried me on, and I was a good fit."

"That true?" Miriam asked Gabriel.

"Could I maybe give you my answer from a standing position?" Gabriel asked politely. "Might be more satisfying to toss me back down if you don't like my answer."

Not looking very pleased, Miriam lifted her foot. Gabriel rose from the floor, rubbing his neck a bit as he stretched his back.

"So?" Joseph asked.

"Joy's right, I married her because she was comfortable. But I never said she was old. I said she wasn't getting any younger, and she should have children." Every eye was now riveted on Gabriel, but Joy didn't feel any relief. She wanted to crawl in a hole and die.

"He said sparks," Blossom said. "Why do you always forget the sparks?"

Gabriel just continued talking. "Joy should have a lot of kids. She's been more of a mother to Sophie than my ex-wife was in Sophie's entire life."

"You don't love Joy?" Miriam reached for his arm, ready to flip him again, but Gabriel stepped out of her reach, moving toward Joy.

"I said, that's why I married her, but it's not the whole truth." He kept moving toward her, his gaze holding hers as tightly as any grip could. Softly, he added, "I didn't realize the whole truth until after the wedding."

"And that would be?" Miriam asked.

"I love her," he answered Miriam, though his gaze never left Joy. "I said she was comfortable and she fit. I worked damned hard at trying to love other women, but I never pulled it off. With Joy, love came easy. So easily that it surprised me to see that she had stolen my heart." His look held Joy's. "I wanted to tell you, but I wasn't sure how."

"I wanted to tell you, but I was afraid you'd laugh. Or

worse, that you'd feel sorry for me," Joy admitted. She felt like laughing and crying, so giddy with the feeling of relief that was flooding her body.

"Ah, hug the girl," Joseph commanded.

Gabriel complied easily. He swept Joy into his arms, and her heart lurched in her chest. He loved her? Was he telling the truth, or just telling her parents what they wanted to hear? Joy looked to the fairies, hoping to find some answer there, but they'd disappeared.

"How 'bout me?" Sophie shouted, racing down the stairs. She evidently felt her father and Joy had forgotten her, because she wormed her way into their embrace.

"How 'bout you?" Joy asked, lifting the girl. "How 'bout this?" She and Gabriel squeezed tight.

"You're squishin' me!" Sophie squealed.

"Should we stop?" Joy asked Gabriel.

"For now, but I think after our company leaves we're going to have to make a Sophie sandwich." He gave them both another squeeze.

"Can I get you all some coffee?" Gabriel asked.

Miriam started to say, "That would be good," but Joseph cut her off. "I think we should leave these two alone for a while. It appears to me they have some talking to do."

"Joseph," Miriam protested. Joy knew her mother loved nothing more than to be in the thick of things.

"Miriam," Joseph said in a voice both women recognized as final. "And, I was thinking that we might borrow our new granddaughter for a while. We'll all go spend the night with Max and Grace, and tomorrow we'll have waffles. Seems to me I recall a little girl who enjoyed waffles with a lot of whip cream on them. She's all grown-up now," he turned and looked at Joy, a mixture of nostalgia and love radiating from his eyes, "so, it's been a while, but maybe someone here might like to go find some?"

"Me?" Sophie asked.

"You. And I hear that Erie has a fine zoo. You know, it's been a long time since I've gone to the zoo." Joseph swung Sophie up into his arms.

"Can we take CheChe, too?" Sophie asked.

"Hm," Joseph appeared to be thinking. "Me, your grandma and our two granddaughters at the zoo? Now, that sounds like a mighty fine plan to me."

Still carrying Sophie, Joseph walked over and hugged Joy. "You be happy, honey," he whispered in her ear.

"I will, Daddy," she said, hugging him back.

Joseph shook Gabriel's hand. "You ever hurt her, and I'm going to make Miriam look like a girly-girl with what I'll do."

"You don't have to worry, sir," Gabriel said.

"Dad. You can call me Dad if you like," Joseph said.

"Mom?" Joy asked. Miriam was staring at the two of them, making Joy more than a little nervous.

"I think the two of you will do," she finally said and swept them both into her arms. "You're going to have to make it up to me that I missed the wedding."

"How do we do that?" Joy asked.

"Well, you're not getting any younger," she said with a twinkle in her eye. "And neither am I. Two granddaughters are all well and good, but you know me, Joy, I'm greedy. I want more."

"And if it was a grandson?" Gabriel asked.

"I raised Nick and Max. Seems I always understood them more than I did my Joy. Guess I could handle another boy or two in the family. Not that I'd mind more girls. I might not understand them as well, but I love them to pieces." With that she kissed Joy and made her escape.

Joy suspected that the glistening in her mother's eyes was unshed tears, but Miriam would have denied it. She never cried, or so she claimed. Truth was, Miriam liked to think she was a tough nut, but in actuality she was Jello. The family loved her enough never to mention her soft side.

They packed an overnight case for Sophie and waved as she left with her new grandparents.

"Well," Gabriel said, shutting the door. "I think your parents were right—we need to talk."

Joy suddenly knew Gabriel had just been mouthing the words her parents wanted to hear. "I'm so sorry," she whispered.

"For what?" he asked, leading her to the couch. When she started to sit beside him, he surprised her by pulling her onto his lap.

"I'm sorry for that scene. My family seems to forget on a regular basis that I'm an adult. I hope you can forget your first meeting with Mom. The rest of the family will be easy."

"Just how big is your family?" Gabriel asked. He toyed with Joy's hair, running his fingers through it.

Joy resisted the urge to lean back and melt into his embrace. They did need to talk, and she needed to keep her wits about her. But keeping her wits about her while she sat on Gabriel's lap and he toyed with her hair was a pretty big task. "There's lots more family. Nick's the last of the immediate family, but there are cousins, uncles—"

"Does your mom have any sisters?" Gabriel stilled.

"Yes. There's my Aunt Sarah and my Aunt Tess."

"And are they anything like her?"

"Oh, no. Aunt Sarah's a gentle soul, but my Aunt Tess, well if you think my mom's tough, you just wait until you meet her." Joy laughed. "Everyone always said I took after Aunt Sarah."

"I think I'm going to like her, but I think I'm going to have to be nervous about meeting your Aunt Tess." He pulled her tighter.

Suddenly, Joy remembered what they'd both said earlier. "About what you said to my family...I want to thank you."

"Thank me?" Gabriel's hand stilled.

"Yes, thank you for telling my mother what she wanted to hear. It will make things so much easier." She shifted nervously in his lap when he said nothing. "And, about what my mother said, what I said, well, I don't want you to worry about it. I mean, my feelings are my responsibility, not yours. I'm sorry. I didn't mean to fall in love with you. It just happened."

"Like hell you are."

"Like hell I am what?" Joy asked, confused.

"Like hell you're sorry about falling in love with me. Why didn't you tell me sooner? I've been so worried that you'd never be able to love me. Oh, I knew you loved Sophie, and the hell of it was, I realized these last few days that I was jealous of my own daughter. It made me feel lower than a worm."

"Jealous?"

"Jealous. God, Joy, I've been so worried you'd never be able to love me." He hugged her to him, and she sank into his embrace, feeling more and more giddy as his confession continued. "When I said you were comfortable, I was right. It just took me a while to realize that the comfort I felt with you was love. I just looked one day and there you were, sitting in the center of my heart. I love you. I don't want you to be sorry for loving me, and I don't want you to ever stop loving me."

He loves me? Truly loves me? He didn't just say it for my mother's benefit? Joy wrapped her arms around his neck and held on for dear life. *He loves me.*

"Stop loving you? There's no chance of that."

Gabriel gave her a little flip, and Joy found herself on her back beneath him on the couch. "Promise me you won't stop."

"I can't stop. I fell in love with you from the start. Even when I thought you were going to marry Helen—even when I thought you only wanted me as a surrogate mother for Sophie—nothing nudged you out of my heart. I can't imagine anything ever will."

"Say the words," he commanded as he began raining his kisses lower and lower. "Say them."

"I love you," Joy said, amazed that she could get the words out. She was finding it hard to breathe, much less talk.

"God, you're beautiful," he murmured.

"Not like Trudi or Helen." Compared to the other women who had been in Gabriel's life, she felt dumpy and undesirable.

Gabriel stopped and looked directly into her eyes. "Honey, you're right. You're nothing like Trudi. I worked at loving her, really worked, but I couldn't do it. That's why my marriage with Trudi fell apart. And I never did manage to love Helen. I told you, we were just friends. But you? You just walked into my life and into my heart like magic. You are the most beautiful woman I've ever seen. I've been drooling over you since the first day we met."

At that moment, Joy felt beautiful. She felt like the most

beautiful creature to ever walk the earth. He loved her. He even drooled over her. The fairies had granted all her wishes, and yes, that was magic. "Thank you," she whispered, sure they would hear her.

And though she saw nothing, three very distinct voices whispered back, "You're welcome."

She kissed her own true love. "Gabriel, you spoke of magic. Well, there's something I should tell you. A bit of a fairy tale."

"Honey, you can tell me anything you want, as long as you keep telling me you love me. You're going to have to tell me every day, as often as you can, for the rest of our lives."

Magic. Maybe the fairies couldn't make people fall in love, but that didn't stop the love she shared with Gabriel from being magic.

He was kissing her, driving every thought except that she loved him from her head.

"You had something to tell me?" Gabriel asked.

"Tomorrow," she promised. "Right now, I want to make some more magic."

At that moment Joy knew that she was where she belonged. In Gabriel's arms, in his heart. It was where she was destined to be. "I love you," she whispered.

"Honey, I love you, too." Gabriel answered.

So wrapped up in the wonder of her fairy tale, Joy didn't even notice the three figures blink from the room.

"Well, that's that," Fern said. "Joy's found her love and her home, and Gabriel has found his Joy."

"See, I kept reminding everyone about the sparks," Blossom said as she stole a quick peek at the couple. "Sparks and drool—it's a winning combination. And those sparks look like they've turned into the raging fire Joy wanted. Yes, we're done. Gabriel's discovered the magic of Joy."

Epilogue

"Now it's time for bed," Max told Sophie.

"Has Santa come yet?" she asked.

"Not while little girls are awake," Grace added. "And CheChe's already sleeping, so Santa's just waiting for you to sleep."

"Marty at school said there was no Santa. But there is, right?"

"Why, that Marty doesn't know a thing. Santa's as real as we are, sweetheart." Once upon a time, Grace didn't believe in fairies, or Santa, or even Glinda the Good Witch, but finding Max with the help of Myrtle, Fern and Blossom had changed her mind.

"Daddy promised to call."

"And he will, sweetheart. He'll call as soon as he can. So, go to sleep," Grace said.

"But they promised. It can't be Christmas if he doesn't come."

"Santa will come," Max promised.

Sophie shook her head. "No, not Santa, my brother."

Grace smiled and stroked the little girl's head. Someday her CheChe would be this big. The thought gave her heart a small tug, but she reminded herself that there would be other babies. Without thinking her hand fell to her stomach. Their newest addition was still too new to show. "What if it's a sister?"

"A brother," Sophie maintained, even as Max scooped her up and carried her up the stairs.

"Oh, it's a brother," Myrtle said merrily.

Three fairy-elves materialized in the living room—one wearing the traditional red velvet, one a traditional green, and one a canary yellow that would never find its way onto any Christmas card.

"I can't help it," Blossom said, too merry to be insulted. "I look best in yellow."

"About Sophie—" Grace started, but Blossom cut her off. "It's a boy."

"You're sure?" Grace asked.

"They're here?" Max groaned as he came back down the stairs.

"Yes, they're here. Now hush. I want to know about the baby," Grace said.

"He's big. Ten pounds, three ounces," Fern said.

"You made sure everything's okay?" Grace asked.

"You know that's not how fairy magic works." Myrtle smiled. "But everything's just fine with mother and son. The father was touch and go for a while. We thought he was going to pass out."

"So, with Joy all settled, we're ready for our biggest cases ever." Fern looked worried.

"We've spent the last few months hammering things out with the fairy council." Myrtle looked as nervous as Fern.

"Hammering out what *things*?" Grace asked. Nervous fairies were dangerous fairies.

"We've been doing a little rewriting of the rules," Fern said casually.

"What?"

"What?" Max asked.

"They've rewritten some of the rules." Now Grace was the nervous one.

Max must have picked up on her nervousness because he took her hand. "What—"

"Shh," she hushed her husband, trying to concentrate on what the fairies were saying. "You've rewritten what rules?"

"Well, now Grace, some of your fairy rules are a bit cumbersome, so we went to the fairy council and got a couple dispensations before we tackled our next cases. This couple's really tough." Myrtle, always the ringleader and boss, uncharacteristically looked to her sisters for support.

"Who?" Grace asked.

"Now, Gracey, you don't have to worry," Blossom soothed.

"Who?" she repeated.

"Nick!" the merry yellow fairy hollered.

"Blossom!" Grace cried.

Blossom gave one of her swooniest smiles. "You see, there's this—"

"Blossom," the other two fairies scolded again.

"Well, let's just say, he's in for his own happily-ever-after," Blossom promised.

With a tinkling of laughter, three fairies dressed as elves blinked out of the room. Only Blossom's voice remained as she said, "And I heard them exclaim, as they blinked out of sight, it's a boy for Joy, and Nick's about to see the light."

"Just what rules do you think they've changed?" Max asked.

"I have no idea, but I'm going to find out. All I can say is, poor Nick." Her mother-in-law had often said it would take a miracle to get playboy Nick to settle down.

Her mother-in-law was wrong. It was going to take *three* miracles—Myrtle, Fern and Blossom.

Poor Nick—but that's another story.

ABOUT THE AUTHOR

Holly lives in Erie, Pennsylvania with her husband, four children and a one-hundred and eighty pound Old English Mastiff. She can't remember a time she didn't read...and read a lot. Writing her own stories just seemed a natural outgrowth of that love. Reading, writing, chauffeuring kids to and from activities makes for a busy life, but it's one she wouldn't trade for any other. She keeps hoping the fairies will come to life and help her, but to date, she's still waiting!

In her "spare" time, Holly loves hearing from her fans. You can visit Holly online at http://members.aol.com/hfur/ or you can reach her by writing Holly Fuhrmann, PO Box 11102, Erie, PA 16514-1102.

Don't Miss

MIRACLE FOR NICK

Coming in 2001

Nick Aaronson is a lawyer who doesn't believe in fairytale romance. He doesn't even believe in fairies, but they believe in him! Myrtle, Fern and Blossom are back, and they have one last Aaronson to find a happily-ever-after mate. And they're determined Nick is going to be happy...whether he wants to be or not.

Glory Chambers thought she was leading the perfect life until she discovers it was a fairytale she'd invented for herself. When a mysterious aunt leaves her a diner in Erie, Pennsylvania, Glory's ready for a new start. But she hadn't planned on Myrtle, Fern and Blossom—they're more adventure than anyone is ready for, even a disgruntled ex-corporate executive. Glory unwittingly hires them and finds that her life is turned upside down when her fairy employees are sued. Who do you hire to represent three fairies in a civil suit? Nick Aaronson, of course!

Thrown together in the fairy-trial of the century, Glory and Nick draw closer, despite their misgivings. A man who doesn't believe in love, a woman looking for independence, and three fairy godmothers determined to matchmake the couple make a dangerous mix. Will Myrtle, Fern and Blossom be able to convince Glory and Nick that they can live happily-ever-after, or will they learn that even magic can't guarantee a...*Miracle for Nick*?